I0763617

First edition, 2026

ISBN: M0D2091113609

Cover design by Mary-ann Sauvage

Independently published.

For Dominique, whose steady support made this possible; for Rachael and Bryan, who never stopped believing in me; and for Matt, my very first sounding board.

The Red Door

By: Mary-Ann Sauavge

Chapter 1 – Morwyn

Hearth & Hollow stood on the corner of Briar Street, its wide front window catching the morning light. Half a block up, directly across the narrow two-way road, the Red Door faced the street without ornament or sign. The bus stop sat between them; its cloudy glass shelter angled toward the street, facing the door. If you stood at the bus stop and turned your head to the right, you could see the café window and the woman who ran it.

People said the café had "always been there," though no one could recall it being built. The bricks were older than the surrounding shops. The wooden beams inside were the kind carpenters no longer made, because the trees they came from no longer grew.

Some said the café felt alive, though they meant it kindly. Warm and comforting. A place where the world seemed to slow down.

Much of that had to do with Morwyn.
There were fine lines at the corners of her eyes, though they did nothing to dull the brightness within them. The backs of her hands bore the quiet map of years, veins faint beneath the skin, yet her movements carried a youthful precision that made guessing her age impossible. Her hair was gathered in a loose bun at the nape of her neck, though a silver strand had long ago decided not to obey it.

On most mornings, the street did not ask to be noticed.

It was a practical sort of place: a stretch of cracked concrete sidewalk bordered by a slouching row of buildings that had seen better decades, a bus stop shelter with cloudy glass, and a coffee shop that smelled like roasted beans and warm sugar from seven in the morning onward.

People walked past. Cars hissed by. The world moved.

And then there was the door.

It stood in the middle of an otherwise blank wall, once too grand for the modest building that held it. Long ago, it must have blazed a bold, glossy crimson. Now the color had faded and dulled, weathered and uneven, the paint lifting in quiet curls along the edges. Time had settled into its grain.

A heavy brass knocker, large as a child's fist, hung slightly crooked. It had long since surrendered its shine, the metal softened to a greened patina like moss on old stone.

No bell. No nameplate. No sign. No one had seen it open in years. It had been still for a very long time. And on this morning, something within it shifted.

She moved through the small shop with ease that made people forget to question it. Some swore she had looked exactly the same for the past twenty years. Others joked she must have the secret to eternal youth.

Morwyn never denied any of it. She simply smiled and poured tea. Her honey cakes soothed hearts in ways medicine could not. Her cinnamon buns stayed warm long after they should have cooled. Her teas seemed to know what each person needed before they tasted them.

People called it intuition, but Morwyn knew better. She didn't predict what people needed; she simply felt it.

In the upper corner of the front window, a spider kept its patient vigil. Morwyn had never brushed away its web. Some things were better left weaving.

This morning, she wiped down the last of the tables, humming softly to herself. She paused at the counter where honey cakes cooled near the window and tipped a thin ribbon of honey over one of them. For a moment, the golden thread curved in a shape almost deliberate. She brushed her thumb lightly against her forefinger… and the shape melted back into smooth sweetness.

Sunlight drifted through the window, catching the dust motes in faint, golden swirls. Outside, the street was waking:

Ray's truck rolling slowly uphill. A student laughed as she hurried past. A boy kicking pebbles along the cracked sidewalk. The soft sound of charcoal scraping upstairs in Sage's studio.

Ordinary people on an ordinary morning. And yet… something hovered beneath it all.

The spider paused mid-spiral. One thread missed its mark by the smallest measure.

Morwyn noticed. She had been expecting this feeling for a long time. She had built her days around avoiding it. Honey cakes, warm cups, small kindnesses, hoping the Weave, like an old wound, would finally stay quiet.

She set down her cloth, and reached for the kettle.

Then it happened…

A pulse. Soft. Warm. Unmistakable. It rolled through the floorboards into the soles of her feet, rising in a single, ancient tremor.

Morwyn inhaled sharply and caught the edge of the counter. Her fingers went numb. That had not happened in years.

"Oh," she whispered. "So, it's begun."

Above the window, the unfinished thread swayed. She walked to the glass. The street looked unchanged. Sunlight spilled across the pavement. People moved about their lives.

But the air felt different. Heavier. Stiller.

As though the world had drawn in a breath and forgotten how to release it.

Morwyn lifted her hand, thumb brushing once more against her forefinger. The wooden sign turned to CLOSED - BE BACK SOON.

She stepped into the light. A thin, unreal brightness coated everything, the kind that sometimes appeared before a storm, when the sky held back its intention.

Morwyn stood still, listening with a deep sense behind her bones. The Weave was shifting. The threads she had watched lie dormant for years were stirring once again.

She felt the tremor again. Not in the ground, but in the space between things. Her gaze drifted to the old door. Usually quiet. Today, it shimmered subtly like a heat ribbon rising from asphalt, invisible to most, bright as a beacon to her.

“The door is awake,” she murmured.

Her pulse flickered with hope, but hope was dangerous. Hope was what had ruined things before.

Morwyn pressed a hand to her shawl, feeling the faint hum of the Weave against her palm. The shifting had begun, and though she could not yet see the pattern, she knew the world was rearranging its threads.

“Not yet,” she whispered into the trembling air. “Please… not yet.” But she already knew.

The Red Door had stirred. The Weave had tightened. And destiny, quiet and patient for so long, had begun to move.

Chapter 2 – Claire

Claire Green sat at the bus stop with her hands wrapped around a paper cup of coffee that had already cooled.

Her bus always ran a little late. For years, she had filled the waiting with scrolling or mentally rehearsing the day ahead, call lights to answer, dressings to change, medications to double-check before rounds began. The endless rhythm of tending and charting and steadying other people's fear. But lately… something had changed.

Her shoulders ached before she reached the clinic. She shifted beneath her coat, already trying to ease the tension.

The little girl who had clung to her hand before surgery yesterday. The elderly man who tried to joke about the pain in his chest. The mother who pretended not to cry. It felt as if the world kept placing more stones in her pockets, expecting her to somehow keep walking.

Today, she found herself looking up at the Red Door.

A chill brushed her skin. She pulled her scarf tighter and leaned back against the cold metal bench. She studied the grand, tired entrance, far too magnificent for the modest buildings crowding it on either side.

Claire closed her eyes.

In her mind, the door opened. Not to fluorescent lights or whispered emergencies, but to a long corridor of cool, veined marble. The air was still and smelled faintly of citrus, touched with the scent of time-worn stone. High arches rose overhead, carved with patterns that caught slivers of sunlight from narrow windows. Sunlight spilled across a thick, silken rug, warm and golden.

Claire pictured herself there, barefoot. The marble felt cool beneath her feet. No rubber soles. No chart to balance. No call light buzzing at her back. Just… space.

In her imagination, she moved slowly, without urgency. She boiled an egg in a quiet kitchen, just one, and arranged it on a small plate with olives, a slice of fresh-baked bread, and a slice of cheese. She carried her simple breakfast to the low table near the window where morning light gathered in soft pools.

Sitting cross-legged on the rug, she ate without rush, without worry, without the clock ticking behind her ribs. She liked that world. She liked it so much that it ached.

Sometimes, she wondered why these daydreams felt familiar, as though she had walked those halls before. As though some part of her already belonged to the quiet inside that imagined home.

Steam from the bus's brakes hissed through her reverie. Claire opened her eyes.

Her bus had arrived. The doors folded open with a tired metallic sigh. Claire stood, tossed the empty coffee cup into the trash can beside the shelter, and glanced once more toward the red door across the street.

Just paint and wood, she told herself.

Then she boarded the bus and let routine carry her away. She always had this irrational feeling that she was leaving something behind.

Chapter 3 – Aaron

Aaron Miller liked walking to school.

Most kids complained about it, the distance, the cold mornings, the long stretch of cracked sidewalk, but Aaron didn't mind. Walking gave him time to imagine and imagining made the rest of the world quieter.

His backpack slung low. His shoelaces were already working themselves loose and, as always, he was kicking a pebble along the pavement, sending it skittering ahead of him like a tiny companion.

He talked to it sometimes, barely audible over the rumble of passing cars.

His imagination was loud, bright, and full of places he wished were real, places where he didn't always feel like the wrong shape for the world. He'd been teased for it many times. Called "weird," "spacey," "storybook boy."

But Aaron didn't mind, mostly. Because imagination made ordinary things magical. And nothing was more magical to him than the Red Door that no one seemed to pay attention to.

He noticed it first years ago. Or at least he thought he had.

A tall, arched door with faded red paint peeling back like petals. A huge brass knocker and doorknob, green with age.

Carvings that looked like vines or waves or flames, never the same shape twice, when Aaron tried to remember them.

Most adults walked past without a glance. And most kids never saw it at all. The world was too busy getting to where it was going.

But every morning, the moment Aaron reached the block where the door stood, something inside him lifted like a magnet pulling a needle.

He always looked up.

This morning was no different.

His pebble bounced directly toward the step in front of the red door and came to rest beside it. Aaron jogged the last couple of steps and stared at the carvings on the wood.

He squinted. "Looks like armor," he murmured, tracing an invisible outline in the air.

He could almost see it, plates of polished metal, overlapping, gleaming once upon a time. In his mind, those carvings were the chest plate of a knight, a knight who lived inside the door and commanded an army of brave warriors.

Sir Walter of the Red Door.

Aaron had invented him. Broad as a wardrobe, loud as thunder, fearless.
Armor black and shining. Boots clattering across stone floors worn smooth by countless battles.

He pictured the knights gathered around a huge table covered in maps and tiny carved figures and castles, dragons and serpents winding between mountains. He imagined them arguing over strategy:

"How do we defeat the dragon that lives in the cove beneath the black cliff?" He smiled at the thought.

"Good luck, Sir Walter," Aaron whispered, giving the air a small salute.

Nothing happened, of course.
The door remained silent.

Aaron bent to pick up his pebble again but froze.

The hair on his arms lifted. Something felt… different. He turned slowly.

The Red Door had shifted. Just slightly, just enough to show the thinnest sliver of darkness between the wood and the frame. There was no sound. That's what frightened him the most.

His heart thudded. He hadn't touched it. He hadn't knocked. He hadn't even said anything loud enough to be heard from the inside.

A faint breath of cool air drifted out from the gap, carrying the scent of damp stone, metal, something ancient.

Aaron took a step closer. "…Hello?" he whispered.

Silence answered him.

The crack was far too narrow to clearly look through.
Nothing moved behind it. The world around him paused, caught between one moment and the next.

Aaron swallowed hard, backing away slowly.

"Just the wind," he whispered to himself. But he didn't believe it.

He kicked his pebble gently, sending it skipping ahead of him down the sidewalk.

He continued toward school, but his heart felt… strange. Light and tingling. And his skin still prickled with goosebumps; he felt as if something had looked back at him.

He didn't see the soft shimmer of the Red Door as it settled closed again. He didn't hear it, the faint, primal sigh of wood.

But he felt it. Deep in his ribs. The door had noticed him. And Aaron, though he didn't know it yet, had noticed the door right back.

Chapter 4 – Sage

Sage Rourke had always seen the world differently. They never quite fit in. When they looked at a room, they did not see furniture; they saw tension and lines.

Some people saw shapes. Some saw colors. Sage saw stories, threads of emotion coiled through everything, waiting to be sketched into existence. It had been that way since childhood.
People joked that Sage's drawings watched them, that the eyes in the portraits shifted when no one was looking. Sage pretended to laugh along, but deep down, part of them wondered if it was true. Lately, though, the gift felt more like a weight than a wonder. If it were gone, they would not know who they were without it.

Sage sat in their studio apartment, a cramped space above a Café and stared at a blank sheet of paper pinned to the easel. Morning light slanted through the windows, catching the silvery chalk dust that floated in lazy spirals.

Nothing came. No shapes tugged at their attention, no colors whispered, and no stories nudged their fingertips.

Sage exhaled sharply and dropped the charcoal stick onto the table. Another day, another frustrating nothing.

The creative block had been growing for months, crawling up from the edges of their confidence like frost on glass. Every time Sage tried to draw, the images felt wrong, flat, lifeless, hollow. The world had always spoken to them in lines and shadows, but now it felt… quiet. Too quiet.

Sage rubbed their palms over their face and stood, stretching the stiffness from their back. The open window let in the crisp morning air, carrying the scent of baking from downstairs and something else, something faint and metallic. Something old.

Sage drifted toward the window without thinking. From here, they could see the street below, people heading to work, a cyclist weaving through traffic, a kid with a backpack too large for his small shoulders. But Sage wasn't watching them.

They were staring at a point down the block where an ancient Red Door stood wedged between two modern buildings like a relic that refused to be forgotten.

The door fascinated them. Sage had sketched it dozens of times. Hundreds, maybe.

Every time, the doorway seemed alive. The carvings changed subtly with each drawing.
The brass knocker seemed to shift angles. The shadows clinging to the doorframe never behaved the same way twice.

Sage thought they were imagining it.

But today? Today, the air around the door shimmered slightly, like heat rising from pavement, except the morning was crisp and cool.

Sage blinked. The shimmer remained. A quiet pulse rippled through Sage's chest, faint but certain, like a drumbeat in the distance. For the first time in weeks, a spark of inspiration flickered. Their fingers twitched, eager for charcoal.

Without looking away, Sage grabbed the nearest sketchbook, flipped it open, and began to draw. The lines came quickly, faster than Sage could think, flowing from some instinct deeper than memory. They tried to slow it down, but the charcoal did not listen.

The Red Door appeared on the page: warped, beautiful, ancient. Then the shadows deepened.

A faint outline emerged, something behind the door. Something waiting. Something watching.

Sage's heart hammered. They lifted the charcoal, staring at what their own hand had produced. "I didn't imagine that," they whispered.

Down the block, the shimmer around the Red Door faded. The street returned to normal. People kept walking. But the spark inside Sage did not go out. For the first time in a very long time, they felt awake, alert, pulled. Something in the world had shifted. And Sage Rourke, artist of living lines, felt the change like a spark racing through their fingertips.

They didn't know what the shift meant. Not yet. But they suspected the Red Door did.

Chapter 5 – Ray

The street had shaken off the last of its early morning sleepiness by the time Ray's truck rumbled up to the curb. The sun had climbed high enough to warm the tops of cars. The coffee shop on the corner, Morwyn's, though the sign simply read Hearth & Hollow, already had a small line of regulars forming outside its green door.

Ray hopped down from the cab with the familiar creak in his knees and tugged on the gloves he kept tucked into his belt. One-man operation, he moved with steady efficiency: bin, lift, clang, empty, roll back. Most people didn't look twice at him. He was part of the background, like the traffic lights or the mailboxes.

He preferred it that way.

Even as a kid, he had been the big quiet presence no one quite knew what to do with. Teachers seated him at the back. Other kids dared each other to touch his arm and run. While other boys stomped through mud or kicked over sandcastles, Ray had been the one kneeling in the sand, rescuing stranded crabs and sea lice and collecting bits of ocean-worn treasure.

A beachcomber at heart.

He'd never grown out of it, only switched beaches for sidewalks and alleyways. Now his treasures came from curbsides and gutters: a lost button, a glass marble, a feather with strange markings, a carved spoon, and the occasional trinket that seemed too unusual to throw away.

"You keep the oddest things, my little Magpie," his mother used to say fondly. She wasn't wrong. He wheeled the trash can from in front of the bus stop back toward its place beside the blank wall.

And the Red Door.

There was always something odd in the trash here. Today it was paper. Not the usual flyers or coffee-stained receipts, but a half-crumpled sheet of thick drawing paper, the kind art students favored. It lay atop of the other trash as if it had been placed there gently.

Ray hesitated, glancing around. No one was watching. The people in front of Morwyn's were busy checking their phones and talking, their breath puffing in the cool air.

He picked up the paper. On it, drawn in charcoal, was the Red Door. The likeness was uncanny. Every curl of peeling paint, every shadow, every tilt of the crooked knocker had been captured with obsessive care. The artist had shaded the cracks in the wood so cleverly that Ray almost felt he could run his fingers along them.

He frowned. There was something else, too, half-erased near the bottom corner. A faint suggestion of a figure sitting at the bus stop, head bowed, hands wrapped around an invisible cup, it felt like seeing proof of a dream he didn't remember.

He brushed his thumb over the ghostly outline and felt a strange tingle along the back of his neck, a sensation like remembering something he was sure had never happened.

"Pretty good, huh?" The voice at his shoulder made him jump. He turned to see Morwyn standing in the doorway of her coffee shop, wiping her hands on a dark apron. Her gray hair was coiled into its usual loose bun at the nape of her neck, wisps escaping to frame a face lined more by smiling than by age.

He held up the drawing, suddenly embarrassed, as if she'd caught him stealing. "It was just on top," he said. "Didn't want it to get ruined if someone meant to keep it."

Morwyn's eyes flicked from the paper to the door and back again. For a heartbeat, something sharpened in her gaze. Something old and measuring.

Then she smiled. "Sage's work," she said. "The artist in the studio upstairs. They throw away more than they sell, I swear. Waste of good paper, if you ask me."

Ray looked back at the drawing. The faint figure at the bus stop tugged at his thoughts.

"You want it?" Morwyn asked.

He thought about saying no. About doing what he usually did, which was mind his business and keep the route moving.

Instead, he heard himself say, "I guess I could hold onto it. Be a shame to crush it with the rest."

Morwyn's smile deepened, the corners of her eyes creasing.

"Then you should," she said softly. "Some things don't like to be thrown away."

Ray wasn't sure if she meant the drawing or something else.

He slid the paper carefully between two flattened cardboard boxes in the front of the truck, where it wouldn't get torn, and finished emptying the bin. When he climbed back into the cab, he checked just once more to make sure the drawing was still there. It was.

Only then did he realize something in the cab had nudged itself open. The small wooden trinket box he kept beneath the passenger seat, the one holding years of found oddities, had cracked open during the drive.

Ray reached down to close it but froze. Inside, the silver sphere sat at the top of the pile, gleaming faintly. He hadn't left it that way.

A soft vibration hummed against the wood just for a moment like the smallest buzzing bee.

Ray swallowed hard. "Okay," he muttered, nudging the box shut. "Not today." He said to no one in particular, "I got work."

But as he put the truck into gear, the sphere buzzed once more. Out on the street, the Red Door watched him leave.

Chapter 6 – Jonas

Jonas had been blind for so long that sight had become a language he no longer spoke. But he saw, oh, he saw. Just not the way others did. Vision was the only way the world could see. Jonas had learned to use all the other senses.

To Jonas, the world lived in vibration, in resonance, in the shifting pressure of sound against air. Footsteps painted outlines. Voices drew silhouettes. The wind sculpted entire landscapes as it moved.

It was more than intuition. More than talent. Music had taught him how to listen deeply enough to see.

He sat now on a carved stone bench beside the old fountain in Briar Park, violin case resting upright beside him like a loyal dog. A violin nuzzled comfortably under his chin. The morning was still tinged with the faint icy hint of colder days to come.

Jonas tuned a single string, plucked it gently, and tilted his head. The air answered back. Something was off today.
A low rumble under everything too faint for most ears, but not for his. A tremor behind the city's steady hum. A shift in the way sound itself moved. Something old had stirred.

The violin case nudged his knee. As it had done in more places than he could remember. Jonas sighed, the sound of someone who had heard this note before. "Yes, yes, I felt it too."

The case nudged him again, impatient this time. He rested his hand atop the worn leather. "You're worse than a terrier who's smelled dinner."

A metallic click sounded from within a language only Jonas and the case understood. "Well, we can't run off just because you're excited,"

Jonas chided lightly. "I say when we leave." The case thumped once in disagreement.

Jonas stood, slinging the violin over one shoulder, picking up the case with the other hand. Vibrations spilled toward him from every direction, guiding his steps even before he took them.

He turned toward the street. And froze. The world trembled bright, sharp, as a tuning fork struck against the bones of the earth. He steadied himself on the edge of the curb.

Someone had brushed the Weave. Someone had touched the threshold.

Jonas inhaled. "So it begins," he murmured. "The Door has chosen."

He crossed Briar Street toward Hearth & Hollow. He didn't need to reach for the handle. Morwyn opened the door before his hand found the air.

"Nice of you to finally join the day," she said. Jonas smirked. "Time is a flexible concept."

"That's exactly what people say when they're late."

Her voice was warm, amused, but underneath it thrummed something taut and alert.

"You felt it too," Jonas said softly. Morwyn nodded once. "One of them brushed the Door. The threads stirred." Jonas's smile faded. "Which one?"

"I don't know yet," Morwyn admitted. "But the air shifted. The Weave woke."

Jonas tapped his fingers lightly on the counter, the rhythm thoughtful. "They're untrained, unaware."

"Everyone is unaware until they're not," she replied. "And the Door doesn't choose lightly."

The violin case shuffled as if it had feet, impatient again.

Morwyn arched an eyebrow. "Does your case need a pastry to calm down?"

"It prefers chaos," Jonas said. The case clicked in agreement.

Morwyn's expression softened, though shadows of worry lingered in her gaze.

"Will you guide them, Jonas?" she asked quietly.

Jonas bowed his head. "I always guide the lost."

He turned toward the door. "They will not walk alone."

He stepped back into the brightening morning, the Weave humming around him like a welcoming chord.

The Red Door waited.

And Jonas walked toward it with a smile only a musician who knows the song before it begins could wear.

Chapter 7 - Claire

Claire had felt the entire day was off since early this morning.

It happened three blocks before her usual stop. The engine coughed, shuddered, and gave a long metallic groan that made every passenger look up. Then the bus rolled to a reluctant halt beside a faded laundromat and a shuttered shoe repair shop.

"Sorry, folks," the driver called back. "She's not going anywhere for a while. You'll have to walk or wait for the next one." A collective sigh rose from rows of tired commuters.

Claire stood slowly, slinging her bag over her shoulder. She considered waiting, but the next bus could be twenty minutes, maybe longer. Walking would only add ten.

She stepped into the cool air, tugging her coat tighter around her. Her breath curled white in the afternoon light. She started down the sidewalk, letting her mind drift into the rare quiet that walking offered, no charts demanding attention, no chiming call lights, no clipped hallway conversations.

Just her and her thoughts. And because her thinking wandered, she walked on aimlessly.

Until she turned her head and saw it.

The Red Door.

Not across the street this time. Not framed by a bus window. Right beside her.

Close enough to see the curls of peeling paint. Close enough to see fine cracks and lines running through the wood. Close enough to see the massive brass knocker greened with age, hung crooked, like a tired eye watching her, and close enough to see something else. The door was slightly ajar. Barely. Just enough to reveal a sliver of darkness.

Claire stopped walking. The world seemed to pause with her. The hum of traffic softened. Even the cold bit a little less sharply at her cheeks.

She looked up and down the street. A jogger trotted past. A delivery van squealed into a parking spot. Someone shouted good-naturedly at a dog. No one looked at the door. No one noticed it was open. No one but her.

She approached slowly, her heart beating faster. She lifted her hand and touched the wood. It was warm. Not from the sun. A deep, steady warmth like something alive beneath the surface. She pulled her hand back, startled.

She should walk away. She had a life built from small, careful motions. Measured breaths and locked doors. She had worked hard for that.

But then a thought whispered up from the quiet place inside her:

What if the inside looks like what you imagine?
What if the marble halls are real?
What if there's a world behind this door that doesn't ask so much of you?

Curiosity got the best of her. Her hand lifted again, almost without permission. She pressed gently against the door. It opened without a sound. The smell hit her first. Not dust. Not rot, But earth… damp and rich. Moss and bark and cool shadows. The scent brought back memories of the woods behind her childhood home after rain, comforting and reassuring.

Air brushed past her, cool and aware. Claire stepped inside. Dim light filtered down from an unseen source, illuminating sandy-colored tiles that yielded under her weight. She crouched, pressed her palm to one. Her instinct was to check, to assess, to understand what she was touching came before thought, it felt smooth and just slightly soft, like damp clay. Her hand came away dry. She straightened, heart pounding.

The foyer opened into a long hallway lined with narrow windows that were little more than slits in the wall allowing thin ribbons of gray light to spill across the floor. Light caught on the air itself, thick with dust particles.

To her left stood an open doorway. Her voice felt trapped behind her teeth for a moment. Then she cleared her throat and said softly:

"Hello?"

Her voice echoed strangely too far, too deep.

No reply.

She tried again, louder: "I don't mean to intrude. Your… your door was open."

Silence answered.

It was not the silence of emptiness. It felt like listening.

Claire took a shaky breath.

"Okay," she whispered, mostly to herself. "Just a quick look. Then I'll go."

She stepped deeper into the foyer.

Through the doorway, a room unfolded a strange gallery of armor. Full metal suits lined the corridor, some polished silver, others dark and dented with age. Chainmail hung like metallic fabric. Shields with unfamiliar emblems rested on hooks. Beautiful antique baroque oil paintings hung from the walls.

Claire approached slowly, mesmerized. She lifted a hand to brush one of the breastplates. It vibrated faintly beneath her fingers with a subtle hum, like the memory of a struck bell. She pulled her hand back.

Then a sound drifted into the room.

"Voices," she said out loud. Distant and muffled. Growing closer.

Claire froze. She was no longer alone.

Then she heard the Red Door close with a soft, certain click.

Chapter 8 - Aaron

Aaron was having an unusually good morning.

He'd found a perfectly smooth stone, round as a marble, and he had been kicking it down the sidewalk like a tiny golden planet rolling ahead of him. The sky was bright. His backpack didn't feel too heavy. He'd even remembered his math homework.

Then the stone veered right. Straight toward the Red Door.

Aaron groaned. "Come on," he muttered, jogging after it. "Not there."

He didn't like getting too close to the door. It wasn't fear exactly, just a prickling at the back of his neck, like stepping beneath motion sensors that knew he was coming before he did.

He stopped a few feet away. His stone had rolled right to the base of the old, faded, peeling door.

"Seriously?" he whispered. He bent to pick it up. And froze. The door…
was breathing**.**

A slow outward push of air, then a soft inward pull, subtle as the shifting of a shadow. A rhythm more felt than seen. As though the old wood inhaled and exhaled by the width of a grain of sand.

Aaron blinked. No... No, that wasn't possible. Things didn't breathe unless they were alive, and doors are not alive.

He straightened.

The green brass knocker lifted just a little.

Aaron's heart thumped in his chest, hard.

He stepped back. The knocker rose higher. He took another step.

The knocker slammed downward with a sharp, thundering **THOCK**, the metallic crack slicing through the morning like a struck gong.

Aaron yelped, stumbling backward so fast he nearly fell.

"Stop it!" he shouted at the door, breath trembling. "I didn't touch you! Leave me alone!"

He clutched his stone tight against his chest.

Silence.

Then faintly, impossibly, "Aaron…"

He froze. Someone had said his name.

Just a whisper. A breathy sound. A voice like wind through old paper.

He backed away until he bumped into the metal trash can.

The door was still again. Closed and innocent. As if nothing had moved at all.

Aaron's lungs felt too small for his body. He didn't run, not yet but, he wanted to. Desperately.

Then a gentle voice drifted across the street:

"Aaron?"

He spun.

Morwyn stood in front of her café, one hand raised in greeting. Her smile was warm, but her eyes…

Her eyes were sharp and full of knowing.

"Are you all right, sweetheart?" Morwyn asked softly.

Aaron swallowed hard.

"Yeah. Fine. Just late."

She studied him for a long moment, deciding whether to press him for the truth.

But she didn't. "Come by after school," she said. "I'll have a cinnamon roll with your name on it." Aaron nodded quickly and hurried off, pulse hammering. Behind him, Morwyn turned her attention toward the Red Door. Her expression changed, the warmth fell away, revealing something older, fiercer.

"You stay away from the boy," she whispered. "Not him. Not yet."

A flake of peeling paint fluttered in response, though no wind touched it. Morwyn felt the Door's answer in her bones.

Chapter 9- Sage

Sage had stopped trusting blank paper.

It wasn't that they lacked ideas. It was that the ideas arrived already formed, complete, insistent, as if they were memories rather than inventions. When Sage sat at the drafting table in the small studio above Hearth & Hollow, charcoal in hand, they often felt less like an artist and more like a conduit. The paper waited. The charcoal waited. And something else waited too.

Sage rubbed their eyes and stared down at the sketch before them.

It was wrong. Not badly drawn, never that. The proportions were precise, the shading meticulous. But the lines didn't behave the way lines were supposed to. They bent subtly when Sage wasn't looking. They thickened in places they didn't remember pressing harder. And the eyes…

Sage swallowed. The eyes followed. They leaned back in their chair, their heart pounding once, sharp and startled. "That's enough," they muttered, setting the charcoal down. "I need air."

The studio was cluttered in the way only a working space could be, half-finished canvases leaned against the walls, shelves bowed under sketchbooks and jars of pencils, scraps of paper littered the floor like shed skins. Every surface bore evidence of obsession.

And every drawing, lately, bore the same subject.

The Red Door.

Sage hadn't meant to draw it the first time. It had simply appeared beneath their hand during a late-night sketch, emerging from shadow with uncanny clarity. Since then, it had found its way into everything: margins, practice sheets, the backs of receipts.

Always the same angle. Always the same patient stillness.

Sage crossed the room, pulled back the curtain covering the window and opened the window. Below, Briar Street hummed quietly. People came and went. Ray's truck idled at the curb. Across the street, the Red Door stood half in shade, half in light. Watching.

Sage's breath caught. They had the sudden, dizzying sensation that the door could see them.

A chime sounded below the café door opening, followed by Morwyn's laugh, warm and familiar. The scent of cinnamon drifted faintly upward through the floorboards. Grounding.

Sage turned back to the sketch, intending to tear it up. Instead, their fingers hovered over the paper. The charcoal lines had shifted again. Not much. Just enough.

Where there had been emptiness behind the door before, now there was depth, a suggestion of space beyond the threshold. A corridor. Shadows layered with light. And there, near the bottom of the page, half-erased but unmistakable…

A shadow figure. Sage hadn't drawn it.

They felt it then, a low hum beneath their skin, a vibration traveling up their spine and settling behind their eyes. Not a sound exactly. It was reverberation. Recognition.

“You’re not supposed to be doing this,” Sage whispered, though they weren’t sure who they were talking to. The figure’s head tilted. Sage pushed back from the table so abruptly that the chair scraped the floor. “No! That was impossible.”

They pressed their palms flat against the worktable, grounding themselves in the familiar grit of charcoal dust and old wood. They told themselves, “You’re just tired. You’ve been working too long”. But the hum didn’t fade. It grew stronger.

Sage grabbed their jacket and keys and fled the studio, taking the stairs two at a time. The café bell chimed as they passed through, Morwyn glancing up in mild surprise.

“Everything all right, love?” she asked. Sage nodded too quickly. “Just… need a walk”. Morwyn watched them go, eyes narrowing slightly.

Outside, the air was crisp and sharp, clearing Sage’s head just enough to keep them upright. They didn’t plan to cross the street.

They didn’t plan to stop. But their feet betrayed them. They found themselves standing across from the Red Door, heart racing, hands tingling.

Up close, it was worse.

The carvings seemed deeper than they should be. The paint peeled in elegant curls. The knocker pulsed faintly, like a sleeping thing, dreaming.

Sage raised a hand. Not to knock. Just to feel.

The moment their fingers brushed the wood, the hum inside them surged, charcoal lines flaring behind their eyes, sketches rearranging themselves in impossible ways.

The door didn’t open. But something opened inside Sage.

A rush of images flooded their mind, ink and fire, threads unraveling, a circle of stone beneath a vast sky. A boy king holding darkness that glowed. A woman walking between breaths. A giant with a shield of light. A blind man smiling as music bent the world. Sage staggered back, gasping. The door fell still.

Closed and Silent.

Sage pressed a hand to their chest, breath shaking.

“I’m losing it,” they whispered. But even as they said it, they knew the truth. They weren’t losing their mind. They were being called.

And whatever waited behind the Red Door, it already knew their name.

Chapter 10 – Ray

Ray slept poorly.

Not because of nightmares, he didn't have those, but because of a low, persistent sense of being noticed. The kind of awareness that kept nudging him awake just as he began to drift, like someone clearing their throat in the dark.

By the time dawn filtered through the blinds, he gave up on sleep entirely.

He shuffled into the kitchen, brewed coffee strong enough to bite back, and leaned against the counter while the kettle clicked and hissed. The quiet felt heavier than usual. Even the refrigerator seemed to hum at a different pitch.

Ray glanced toward the top shelf. The wooden trinket box sat exactly where he'd left it. As he found himself approaching the box, he told himself, "Do not to look inside," but he looked anyway.

The lid lifted easily as if it had been waiting. Inside, the familiar collection lay undisturbed, the buttons, the glass marble, the carved spoon, until his gaze landed on the silver sphere. It was no longer tightly closed.

Ray frowned, reached out and picked it up with his thumb and forefinger.

The vibration started immediately.

A steady, pulsing thrum that traveled up his arm and settled behind his sternum, deep and unsettling.

“Huh,” he murmured. “That’s new.”

Ray put the sphere back into the box. The carvings on the sphere shifted.

Ray blinked hard. The symbols were moving and aligning, sliding into patterns that made a strange, intuitive sense, like a lock recognizing the right key.

The sphere rolled, just slightly, until it rested against the inner edge of the box. There was a soft click.

Ray leaned closer. A seam appeared. So fine it might have been imagined, except it wasn’t there before.

His heart began to race, though his hands stayed steady. Ray had always been like that. Fear arrived late for him, if it arrived at all. He had spent his life picking up what others dropped. The strange rarely startled him.

He lifted the sphere. It warmed further in his palm. “Okay,” he said quietly. “Easy now.” The seam widened. With a gentle, almost polite sound, the sphere unfolded, segmented, petal by petal, revealing a hollow center.

Inside lay two things. A fleck of red paint that curled elegantly. And beneath it, a dark red gem, not glass but crystal. Something older, denser, seemed to have weight beyond its size.

Ray exhaled slowly. “Well,” he said. “You’re definitely not normal.”

The ruby pulsed once, answering him. The vibration intensified, spreading outward, rippling through the kitchen. Glassware chimed softly in the cupboard. The floor hummed beneath his boots. Ray felt it then, not danger, but direction. Like a hand at his back pushing him slightly.

He closed the sphere carefully, the segments folding back into place with a satisfied click. The vibration faded, leaving behind a quiet certainty. Something had changed. For the first time, his collecting no longer felt accidental.

Later that morning, as Ray drove his route, the city felt… thinner. Sounds carried farther. Colors seemed sharper. And every time he passed Briar Street, the sphere vibrated in the box beneath his seat.

By mid-morning, he found himself slowing the truck without deciding to. The Red Door stood ahead.

Ray parked. He didn't get out. He rested his hands on the steering wheel, breathing deeply. "I hear you," he said aloud. The vibration answered

Chapter 11- Claire Enters the Door

The door closed behind her with a definite click. Claire spun, heart racing, and reached for the handle. It didn't budge. It wasn't simply locked; it was absent. The door was still there, but the idea of opening it had gone. Her breath came too fast. "Okay," she whispered. "Okay, that's… fine. I'm fine, just breathe."

The faint woodland scent lingered, steadying her just enough to keep her from panicking. She pressed her palms together, grounding herself the way she did with patients in crisis. Slow in…. slow out.

The voices she'd heard earlier drifted again through the space, indistinct, overlapping, too far away to understand. They echoed oddly, as if the walls bent the sound on purpose.

Claire took a cautious step forward. The tiles beneath her feet yielded slightly, warm and forgiving, nothing like the cold hardness she'd expected. With every step, the hallway seemed to lengthen ahead of her, stretching just beyond reach.

The narrow windows lining the walls pulsed faintly as she passed, light waxing and waning like the breath of lungs. She stopped.

"Hello?" she called again, more firmly this time. "Is anyone here?"

Her own voice echoed back to her, changed, softer, layered.

"Yes."

The words weren't spoken aloud. It bloomed in her mind. Claire staggered, clutching the wall.

"You came." The voice continued.

The presence wasn't threatening. It felt attentive. Claire swallowed hard. "I didn't mean to intrude. I was just... curious."

A pause. Then the hallway shifted. The stone softened, seams melting into one another. The narrow windows widened, light spilling inward until the corridor opened into something vast. Revealing a beautiful, lush garden. Claire stepped forward without realizing she'd moved.

Grass brushed her ankles, cool and dew-damp. A stone path curved through flowering shrubs and low trees, their leaves shimmering as if woven from sunlight. Birds flitted between branches, their calls gentle, layered with the buzzing of insects and the murmur of water. Fragrant, beautiful flowers spilled in every direction.

At the garden's center stood a table. It was set for two. White linen stirred in a breeze she couldn't feel on her skin. A teapot steamed softly. Two cups waited. Everything was impossibly peaceful, achingly so.

Claire's chest tightened. "This isn't real," she whispered.

"It is as real as you are," the presence replied.

She approached the table slowly, hands trembling. The chair pulled back slightly, inviting her to sit.

She didn't. Instead, she pressed a hand to her sternum. "I shouldn't be here," she said. "I need to get home …."

"You have nowhere to be right now." The presence said.

The words struck harder than any accusation. Images flickered and swirled around her like mist; hospital rooms, dim lights, the steady rhythm of monitors. Faces blurred by grief. Hands she'd held while machines beeped their final insistence. She felt nauseous.

"What is happening?" she asked, her breath shortening.

"You stayed when others left. You took their fear; you held on to their suffering; you did not let it pass through."

Claire's knees buckled. She dropped to the floor, breath shuddering.

"That's not true," she whispered with a hint of anger. "I'm just… tired."

"Yes." The voice agreed.

The garden dimmed slightly, shadows lengthening.

"You were never meant to carry it alone."

"What? Who?" She asked, confused.

Something rustled behind her. Claire spun, startled. From behind the sweeping branches of a willow tree stepped a figure tall and radiant, their form indistinct at first, light and iridescent, shaped like a person rather than flesh. As it moved closer, features sharpened: strong lines, calm eyes, a presence that radiated steadiness.

Recognition struck Claire so suddenly that it stole her breath.

"No," she breathed. "You can't be…"

The figure smiled gently. "In your world," he said, his voice layered with warmth and gravity, "I was called Caleb."

Her throat closed. The patient who couldn't be save. The one who smiled at her even as he slipped away. The one whose passing had haunted her longest. Here, I'm called "Kaelith," he said softly.

Claire pressed her hands to her face, tears spilling freely now. “I failed you.” Kaelith shook his head. “You guided me,” he said. “You stood at the crossing when I could not walk it alone.” She looked up, shaking. “I don’t understand.” “You will,” he replied. “But first, you must rest.”

He gestured to the chair across from her. “For once,” Kaelith added gently, “let someone hold your fear.” The garden breathed around them. And for the first time in years, Claire rose from the floor and let herself sit.

Chapter 12 – Aaron and Morwyn

The last bell of the school day rang with a shrill, relieved clang, and Aaron burst through the front doors with the rest of the students. Backpacks bounced. Voices overlapped, and a soccer ball sailed across the field. The ordinary chaos of dismissal.

Aaron liked this moment, the feeling of being released, like a balloon stretched to the max just before it burst. But today, something felt… off. The sunlight looked strange. A little too golden and a little too thick. Like the air itself had texture. He shook it off and started down the sidewalk, kicking a pebble out ahead of him. He chose a different path today, not wanting to go near the Red Door again after what happened that morning. His backpack thumped against his side. He looked up when he reached Morwyn's café.

There she was, waiting outside the door, a warm paper bag in hand, her shawl wrapped loosely around her shoulders. "Afternoon, sweetheart," she called as he approached. "I've got something for you." Aaron tried not to smile too big. "You really made one for me?" "I made three," Morwyn said with a grin, "But I burned one and ate another out of spite; this one survived." She held out the bag. The smell hit him immediately; cinnamon, sugar, and freshly baked dough. His favorite. Aaron took the bag hungrily. "Thanks."

Morwyn gently rested her hand briefly on his shoulder and said, "Come sit with me a moment." Aaron blinked. She didn't usually invite him to sit. But he followed her to the small café table just outside the door. The sun warmed the wooden surface, and birds hoped hopefully hopped near their feet.

Aaron opened the bag and tore off a piece of the bun, savoring the first bite. Morwyn watched him with soft eyes that seemed older today… heavier.

"So," she began lightly, "how was school?"

"Fine."

"Anything strange happen?"

Aaron froze mid-chew. He swallowed.

"Like what?" he asked, trying to sound casual.

Morwyn folded her hands atop the table.

"Oh, I don't know," she said with a shrug. "Strange feelings, strange sights, strange… knocks."

Aaron's stomach dropped. He stared at her, wide-eyed.

She knew. Maybe not everything, but she knew something had happened.

He looked down at the cinnamon bun, picking at a corner.

"The door knocked at me," he whispered. "This morning. I didn't knock first. It just… did it."

Morwyn nodded once, as if she had expected this answer. "Did it frighten you?"

"Yes," he admitted quietly.

She hummed thoughtfully. “Good, fear is a sensible reaction to things that are older and smarter than we are.”

Aaron looked up sharply. “What does that mean?”

Morwyn’s lips curved in a knowing smile. “It means,” she said slowly, “that the world is sometimes bigger than people pretend, and there are things in this world we don’t understand. It also means that some things in it… choose who they speak to.”

“Why me?” Aaron asked, voice cracking just a little.

Morwyn reached over and smoothed his hair gently to the side, the way a grandmother might.

“Because you listen,” she said. “Because you imagine and because you see things as they could be, not only as they are”.

“That’s bad?”

“No,” she whispered. “It’s beautiful.”

Her face softened further. “But it’s dangerous if you walk toward something before you understand it.”

Aaron swallowed hard.

“Good boy. Finish your bun.”

He took a bite to appease her, though his stomach churned.

After a moment, he asked, “Morwyn?”

“Yes?”

“You said some things choose who they speak to. Does the door do that?”

Her gaze drifted toward the old building across the street.

"Yes," she said softly. "It does."

"And it chose me?"

She looked back at him, and though her smile remained gentle, her voice was steady.

"It has taken notice of you," she said. "That is not the same as choosing."

Aaron let out a shaky breath. "But could it choose me?"

Morwyn closed her eyes briefly, as if offering a silent prayer. "Yes," she whispered. "It could."

A chill ran down Aaron's spine, despite the warm sunlight.

Aaron cradled what was left of the warm cinnamon bun as Morwyn suddenly inhaled, her eyes sharpening with decision.

"Wait here," she murmured, already rising from her chair.

He watched her disappear into the café and return moments later holding a small object wrapped in soft, worn linen. She set it gently on the table.

"I've been saving this," she said quietly. "For someone who would need it."

Aaron's fingers trembled slightly as he unwrapped the linen.

Inside lay an obsidian arrowhead, sleek, glassy-black, shimmering with silvery flecks that flickered when they caught the light.

Aaron's breath left him in a wide-eyed whisper. "It's beautiful…" Morwyn nodded slowly.

"Obsidian is its proper name," she said, "but some of us… old-timers… prefer a different one."

She leaned closer, voice dropping to a near-whisper, "Dragon glass."

Aaron's heart thumped. "That sounds… magical and dangerous."

Morwyn smiled softly. "Only if misused. Dragon glass is forged in volcanoes so hot it changes truth into stone. It remembers things. It listens, and it can tell bravery from fear."

He rolled the arrowhead gently across his palm. It was cool… but felt warm in the center, like it had a heart buried deep inside.

"What's it for?" he asked. Morwyn folded his fingers around it. "For courage," she said. "For when the world feels too big, and shadows feel too close. When something calls your name, and you're not sure if you should answer."

Aaron swallowed. "Should I… stay away from the door?"

Morwyn hesitated, not with uncertainty, but with honesty trying to soften itself for a child.

"I want you safe," she said. "But fate listens poorly to warnings. So instead… take this."
She tapped his closed hand.
"When you're afraid, hold it tight, point downward, toward the ground, always."

"Why downward?" Aaron asked.

Morwyn's expression flickered, a shadow of memory crossing her features.

"Because dragon glass responds," she said. "You want it listening, not cutting. It can draw courage out of you… and sometimes, something else."

"Something else?" Aaron echoed. She gently touched his closed hand, motherly. "There are old stories," she said softly. "Stories of guardians bound to flame and truth, protectors that once answered to those who carried dragon glass."

"Guardians like… dragons?" Aaron whispered. Her eyes softened into a smile. "Perhaps," she said. "But those are tales for another day."

He placed the arrowhead carefully into the small pocket of his backpack, the one he never used; it fit perfectly as if it had been waiting for that spot.

Aaron looked up again. "Morwyn?"

"Yes, dear?" "If this came from a guardian… does that mean someone gave it to you first?" he asked with a wonder in his eyes.

Morwyn's gaze drifted toward the Red Door, her voice turning gentle with old wisdom.

"Yes," she whispered. "A very long time ago." "Did it help you?" he enquired.

"It saved my life," she said.

A chill slid down Aaron's spine. Morwyn stood, straightened her shawl, and nodded toward the road.

"Go on, now. And remember: if anything strange happens, anything at all, you come straight to me."

"Okay," Aaron said, voice small but steady.

He walked away, the warm bun in his hand and the cool weight of dragon glass pressing lightly against his lower back.

Across the street, the Red Door remained still.

But deep inside its wooden bones, something ancient turned its gaze toward the boy now carrying a shard of dragon glass, a claim and a promise. Someday… a summons.

Chapter 13 - Aaron Enters the Door

Aaron lay awake, tracing every crack in the ceiling. Every time he closed his eyes, he heard the sound again, but he did not feel afraid; he felt unusually calm and certain. But the knock…and worse than the knock was the whisper of his name.

By the time the pale gray light of morning crept through his curtains, he was already awake, staring at the ceiling, the dragon glass warm in his fist. He hadn't meant to keep holding it all night. But every time he loosened his grip, the unease returned, sharp and buzzing, so he'd wrapped his fingers around it again and drifted into shallow, restless half-sleep.

He slipped out of bed quietly, dressed without waking his parents, and ate toast that tasted like nothing. His backpack stayed by the door. This wasn't a school morning.

The street was still sleepy when Aaron stepped outside. Dew clung to the grass. The air smelled clean and new after the night's rain. His feet carried him where they wanted him to go. Briar Street.

The Red Door stood ahead, unchanged and waiting. Aaron stopped a few steps away. It wasn't breathing now, it wasn't moving, it was simply there.

He reached into his pocket and pulled out the dragon glass arrowhead. In the soft morning light, it looked darker than before, black as ink, edged with a faint red glow that looked like embers.

Aaron hesitated, "Okay," Aaron whispered. "I'm here". The knocker did not lift. The door did not creak. Instead, the dragon glass warmed sharply in his hand, insistent. The air around the door shimmered.

Aaron took a breath. He knocked once...

The sound was softer than he expected, more like knocking on old bone than wood.

The door opened immediately. No drama, no resistance, just a smooth, welcoming inward swing.

Aaron's heart thudded. The smell reached him first: earth, damp leaves, and weathered wood. Familiar and strange all at once.

He hesitated at the threshold. "What if I can't come back?" he whispered. The dragon glass pulsed. "For courage." Morwyn's voice echoed in his memory, steady and sure.

Aaron squared his shoulders. "I'm not a baby," he muttered to the door, to himself, to whatever listened. And he stepped inside. The door closed behind him with a soft, final hush.

The world beyond was dim. The floor beneath his sneakers felt slightly springy, like packed sand at the edge of the sea. Narrow windows lined the walls, letting in pale ribbons of light that shifted as he moved.

"A hallway," Aaron breathed. "Cool."

He walked deeper, curiosity pushing fear aside in careful steps. The space widened suddenly, opening into a vast chamber, and Aaron forgot how to breathe.

Suits of armor lined the walls, dozens of them, polished silver, darkened steel, leather, and chainmail. Shields bore unfamiliar symbols. Weapons rested peacefully on racks, as if waiting for stories rather than war.

"Whoa ….I was right, "This is amazing," he said in awe.

A sound stirred near the far end of the room. A soft snort.

Aaron spun. Something moved in the shadows, small, clumsy, unmistakably alive.

Two yellow glowing eyes blinked open. A creature no bigger than a large puppy dog shuffled forward, scales catching the dim light like embers under ash. Smoke puffed gently from its nostrils as it sneezed.

Aaron stared. The creature tilted its head. They regarded each other in stunned silence. Then the creature tripped over its own tail and tumbled sideways with a surprised huff.

Aaron burst out laughing before he could stop himself. "Oh my god," he breathed. "You're not scary at all."

The little dragon scrambled upright, affronted, and puffed a tiny flame that fizzled harmlessly in the air. The dragon glass in Aaron's hand flared warmly.

The dragon's eyes widened. Recognition passed between them quickly and deeply. The creature padded forward and pressed its forehead gently against Aaron's shin.

Aaron swallowed hard, his laughter fading into something softer.

"Hi," he whispered. "Are you all alone?" he said, looking around the chamber. "I guess… I guess it's just us, then."

The dragon chirped, tail wagging. Somewhere deep within the Door, something ancient stirred.

Chapter 14 – Ray enters the door

Ray parked the truck a little way up from the Red Door and turned off the engine. The sudden quiet rang in his ears. He sat there longer than he meant to, hands resting on the steering wheel, breathing slow and steady. The wooden trinket box sat on the passenger seat beside him, lid closed and silent.

"You're not supposed to rush things," Ray muttered, though he wasn't sure who he was talking to… Himself, maybe, or the strange pull that had followed him all morning like a hand at his back, gently guiding him.

The Red Door waited down the street.

It looked the same as always. Faded, ordinary, and patient. Ray reached for the trinket box and opened it. The silver sphere was awake.

He lifted it carefully. The familiar vibration answered immediately, spreading through his palm and up his arm, settling deep in his chest where his breath lived.

"Yeah," he said quietly. "I feel it too."

The seam appeared again, faint but certain. Ray didn't flinch this time. He turned the sphere in his hands, thumbs, finding the subtle grooves as if they had always belonged there. The segments shifted smoothly, unfolding with a soft, almost respectful sound.

The ruby inside pulsed once. A notch appeared on the inner surface of the sphere, a shallow hollow shape, not for decoration, he assumed, but for a purpose.

Ray hesitated for only a moment before pressing the ruby into place. The moment it seated, the vibration deepened, no longer a hum, but a steady resonant vibration. The silver petals folded inward again, reshaping themselves.

Ray stepped out of the truck. The street felt thinner than before, like a place between places. Sound dulled, and the light softened. Even the air seemed to wait. Ray did not realize he still had the sphere in his hand.

He crossed halfway toward the Red Door and stopped. Something moved at the edge of his vision. A small boy, moving quickly, his hood up and shoulders tense. The kid hesitated at the threshold, just long enough for Ray's chest to tighten.

"Hey…." Ray called out instinctively.

The door opened. The boy slipped inside, and the door closed again, smooth, silent, final.

Ray stood frozen. Had he really seen that?

The street looked normal again. A car passed. Somewhere, a phone rang, with no sign of anything unusual.

But Ray's hands had already curled into fists.

A familiar pressure settled behind his ribs, the same one he'd felt his whole life, whenever something smaller than him needed standing up for.

“Damn it,” he muttered. He didn’t know the kid, but he recognized him from the streets. Didn’t know where he’d gone and didn’t know what waited behind that door. But he knew one thing with bone-deep certainty:

No child should walk into something that feels so uncertain alone. Ray tightened his grip on the silver sphere.

The seam appeared immediately. Ray approached the door, and the door seemed to give way too easily; it swung open. Darkness spilled out, cool and thick as mist. Ray choked on the air. “No turning back, now huh,” he whispered.

He slipped the sphere into his pocket and stepped inside. The door closed behind him, and the world changed.

The street was gone. The truck, the streetlights, the boy's small frame disappearing into shadow, all of it, erased. Ray stood in absolute darkness. His breath came fast, too loud in his own ears. The air was different here, cool, dense, pressing against his skin like water. He could feel the space around him, massive and waiting, though he couldn't see a thing.

The sphere in his pocket burned warm. Ray's hand shot to it instinctively, fingers closing around it. Its heat steadied him just enough to stop the panic clawing up his throat.

"Kid?" he called. His voice didn't echo. It was swallowed whole. Ray blinked hard, trying to force his eyes to adjust. And slowly, so slowly, it might have been his imagination, shapes began to form in the darkness. A presence. Something tall and still. The silhouette didn't move closer. It simply was vast, patient, waiting in a way that made Ray's knees want to buckle.

He forced himself to breathe. "Okay," he whispered. "Okay. Kid's in here somewhere. Just… keep moving." The darkness didn't answer, but his eyes began to adjust. Ray took a step. Then another. The air condensed and became heavy. Old, like stepping into a space that had been sealed for centuries and was only now remembering how to hold a living thing.

The sphere in his pocket pulsed slowly and steadily. Ray kept walking. Shapes of armor began to emerge, and soft stone beneath his feet. Walls curved upward, arches that bent in ways architecture shouldn't allow. And scattered throughout the space were objects, so many objects. Broken things. Lost things. Things that had mattered once and been forgotten.

Ray's chest tightened. This place knew him. The silhouette faded as the chamber came into focus, dissolving into the architecture itself, as if it had been the room's only way of looking back at the center. Something waited.

Ray stopped when he reached the center of the chamber. Here, on a pedestal carved from blackened Damascus iron, lay a single object: a circular metal disk. Simple, plain. Yet glowing faintly.

Ray felt a sudden pressure in his chest, not fear, but something like emotion without words. He stepped closer. The disk wasn't shiny or ornate. It wasn't even attractive. Just a circle of dull metal with three faint overlapping marks carved into it.

Ray whispered, "Holy… crap." The Sphere in his pocket glowed sharply in response. Ray reached out, fingers trembling, but before he touched it, the shield lifted, ever so slightly, as if wanting to avoid being touched.

Ray froze. "Okay, you don't want to be touched, got it, but I'm not sure what I'm supposed to do now?" The shield tilted, as if unconvinced. "I'm a trash collector," Ray murmured. "I pick up weird stuff sometimes, sure, I'm good at it. But this? I wouldn't even know where to start."

The shield lowered again… gently. As if understanding.

Ray stared at it, throat tight. "You're… waiting for… me, aren't you?" The sphere pulsed hard enough to warm his thigh. Ray let out a shaky laugh. “Okay, okay, but slow. Let’s not do any floating weapons or exploding magic. I’m new to this.”

He lifted his hand out of his pocket, he unfolded his fingers, and the Ruby flew out of the sphere towards the shield; the shield rose to meet it. Ray’s arm was still extended, and the shield shifted forward to meet it. Their contact was soft like touching warm iron that had cooled after being forged. Ray felt something inside the shield recognized something inside him. A connection of strength, care, and gentleness disguised by size. A Protector.

The shield illuminated slightly, not glowing fully, just a flicker, like dim embers. Ray’s breath caught. “Why does this feel like I’ve held you before?” A faint whisper echoed through the chamber. Memory, Ray staggered, gripping the shield tighter.

He saw flashes, holding this object before, in another life, standing between danger and those who couldn’t defend themselves, lifting walls with his bare hands, lifting people from rubble, lifting… friends. Ray gasped and blinked hard. The memory faded.

The shield rested on his arm now, quiet and waiting. “Okay,” Ray whispered. “Okay. I think I got it. Maybe just a little.” The shield hummed once, a low, comforting vibration, and Ray felt something slip into place inside him. Ray turned when he heard a distant door click closed and a child laughing, “Kid,” he thought.

·III·

Chapter 15 – Sage Enters the Door

Sage noticed the line because it didn't belong. It ran straight along the studio floor, dark and precise, as if someone had dragged a stick of charcoal across the wood and forgotten to stop. It cut through dust and old paint splatters without smudging, uninterrupted by cracks or grain.

Sage froze, breath held, they hadn't drawn it, the line hadn't been there a moment ago.

Slowly, cautiously, Sage knelt and touched it with one fingertip. It was charcoal. They felt a buzz in their fingertips. The line was alive. The line buzzed once beneath their skin, then continued moving. Sage jerked their hand back as the charcoal mark slid forward, inch by inch, flowing across the floor with deliberate purpose. It reached the wall, didn't pause, and it then slipped beneath the baseboard through a crack.

"No," Sage whispered. "That's not how lines work." But the line didn't care. It reappeared on the stairwell wall, climbing upward at an impossible angle, bending around corners, always leading down towards the door, toward the street. Sage followed. They didn't grab a jacket. Didn't lock the studio, they didn't look back when Morwyn glanced up from the café below, brows knitting with concern.

Outside, the charcoal line stretched across the sidewalk, stark against the concrete. No one else noticed it, people stepped over it without seeing it, feet passing straight through as if it weren't there at all, only Sage could see it.

The line led directly to the Red Door.

Sage stopped inches from it, heart racing, but the charcoal mark didn't stop; it slipped beneath the door. Sage swallowed. "This is a terrible idea," they whispered. They could just go back upstairs and pretend none of this was happening.

The line buzzed with a quiet insistence. Sage reached out, fingers brushing the door's surface. They pushed and the door opened. The charcoal line flowed forward, spilling into the hallway beyond, curling over the warm stone floor, threading its way into the dim interior las it had always belonged there.

Sage stepped across the threshold. The door closed behind them with a soft, knowing hush.

Inside, the hallway breathed gently, narrow windows spilling pale ribbons of light. The charcoal line stretched onward, guiding Sage deeper, never wavering. It led them into a chamber of stone columns arranged in a hexagon. The line climbed one column and stopped. The stone shuddered.

Etchings emerged slowly, lines carving themselves into the granite, precise, intentional. A long, slender shape took form: graphite-dark, unmistakable. A mark-maker.

Sage exhaled, and something inside them settled. "I see," they whispered. The charcoal line shimmered, then it lifted, peeling away from the stone, drifting upward like smoke reversing its path. Sage watched, transfixed, as the line coiled in the air between them and the column, then it gently settled in their open palm like a tattoo. It then sank in under their skin, causing them to feel unsteady and suddenly be able to see the grid in the air.

The symbol on the column pulsed once, then stilled. Sage closed their hand slowly, feeling the line electric beneath their skin now interwoven. A new sense, a new way of seeing and understanding.

They hadn't been dragged here. They hadn't been tricked. They had followed a line only they could see, and now that line lived inside them. Had they made the right choice?

Chapter 16 – Aaron and the Dragon

Aaron stared at the dragon. The dragon stared back. Its wings rustled, folding and unfolding as if it were trying to remember how they worked.

Then it yawned a wide, toothy yawn that showed rows of tiny, needle-sharp teeth and a flicker of ember-glow at the back of its throat. Aaron couldn't help it. He laughed.

The dragon's eyes brightened. It made a curious chirping sound and padded closer, stretching its neck to sniff at the dragon glass still clutched in Aaron's hand.

"You, uh… You made this?" Aaron asked, holding it up. The dragon huffed proudly, unmistakable and bumped its snout against his palm. "Okay," Aaron said, voice steadier now. "So… what now?"

The dragon turned abruptly and trotted toward the far side of the chamber, glancing back as if to say, "Well? Are you coming?"

Aaron followed.

The chamber was larger than he'd realized. Stone pillars carved with symbols rose toward a vaulted ceiling, and along the walls, alcoves glowed faintly with trapped light. The dragon moved with purpose, sniffing at corners, pawing at cracks in the stone, occasionally letting out a curious trill.

“What are you looking for?” Aaron asked. The dragon stopped in front of a carved panel on the wall and scratched at it. Aaron knelt beside it. The panel showed five symbols arranged in a circle, a flame, a wave, a leaf, a star, and a spiral.

In the center was a shallow depression, shaped like a handprint. “Is this… the way out?” Aaron asked. The dragon huffed and head-butted his knee. “Okay, okay, so we need to do something.” Aaron pressed his hand into the depression.

Nothing happened. The dragon made a sound that could only be described as a sigh. Aaron frowned. “You got a better idea?” The dragon turned and scampered toward one of the alcoves. It pawed at something on the ground, then looked back expectantly.

Aaron walked over. Scattered across the floor of the alcove were five small stones, each one glowing faintly with a different color: red, blue, green, silver, and gold.

“Oh,” Aaron said. “We need to put these in the right spots.” The dragon chirped in agreement, already nosing at the red stone. It should have been simple. It was not. The dragon had opinions.

Aaron picked up the blue stone and moved toward the wave symbol. The dragon immediately blocked his path, wings flaring. “What? This one's obviously water.” The dragon shook its head and nudged the blue stone toward the spiral instead. “That doesn't make sense,” Aaron muttered. But he placed it there anyway. The stone clicked into place, glowing brighter. “Okay, fine. You were right.” The dragon puffed out its chest, visibly smug. Aaron grinned despite himself. “Don't let it go to your head.”

They worked through the rest together, Aaron guessing, the dragon correcting, occasionally knocking a stone out of his hand when he was about to make a mistake. By the time they placed the final stone (the silver one, which Aaron had been certain went with the star but the dragon insisted belonged to the flame), Aaron was laughing. "You're kind of bossy, you know that?" The dragon trilled proudly.

The panel glowed. The symbols lit up one by one, and with a deep, resonant hum, the wall split apart, revealing a passageway lined with soft golden light. Aaron stood, brushing dust off his knees. The dragon circled his legs once, then darted toward the passage. It stopped at the threshold and looked back….Waiting.

Chapter 17 - Morwyn

Morwyn stood alone across the street, the Red Door closed and still. She felt Aaron inside.
She felt Ray enter moments later. She felt Sage's Mark ignite in the realm itself. She felt Claire crossing thresholds unseen. The Weave trembled like a net pulled too tight.

Morwyn wiped sweat from her brow. "Too many at once," she whispered. "Too many threads pulling." She moved quickly into the café. To the back room. She opened the old wooden chest with shaking hands, she had sworn never to open again, the last time had cost her dearly. But promises don't survive fate. Inside the chest lay the sacred tools of her lineage:

- A silver-threaded circlet
- A vial of moon water
- A coil of red twine
- A pinch of iron dust
- A white candle that had never burned
- And the black dragon scale, vibrating fiercely now

Morwyn drew a circle on the floor with salt, and with chalk drew one symbol for each of the five souls:

 Claire

 Sage

 Aaron

 Ray

And one empty mark… waiting for the fifth, Jonas – The guide, like he had done so many times through the ages.

She placed the candle in the center. It lit itself. The flame shot upward, shimmering violet. Morwyn spoke the words she had sworn never to use again:

“Guard them in shadow,
Guide them in light.
Bind their paths, bind their fate,
Till all is set right.

Shield their breath through depths unknown,
Hold the line where threads are thrown.
Five chosen. Five threads. One Weave
Be shown”.

The chalk symbols glowed. The flame roared. The dragon scale vibrated until it hummed like metal singing. Morwyn’s eyes filled with tears. “Oh my brave ones,” she whispered. “Whatever waits for you in there… may the old powers walk beside you.”

She pressed her palm to the floor. A wave of shimmering golden energy shot outward through the café, across the street, under the Red Door, and vanished into the realm beyond it. Morwyn sagged, exhausted. “It’s begun,” she whispered. “The Five have entered.”

Chapter 18- Ray

Ray hadn't panicked when he entered the Red Door. Although he really wanted to. His whole body suggested it. But his throat, being loyal in all the wrong ways, refused to make more than a muffled squeak. His voice cracked halfway through "fantastic, I'm afraid, but I'm still moving, that's always good." He was breathing heavily when he entered the chamber, yet he wasn't alarmed when the shield began to move; all he felt was calmness. But now he felt very unsure of where to go. The shield now on his arm made him feel a little safer …

Somewhere in the dark, something rumbled. Ray's knees wobbled. "Nope," he said. "Absolutely not. I reject this entire situation." Then a single, clean violin note sliced through the dark.

Ray jerked upright.

The note was soft, gentle like a hand resting on his shoulder, saying, "Hold on now. Let's not panic yet".

The darkness shifted. Something was approaching. Footsteps, calm, slow, unbothered. Ray whispered to himself, "Please be friendly. Please be friendly. Please don't be a demon with a violin…"

A laugh and a voice cut through the dark: "Well, I'm flattered you think I could manage a violin if I were a demon."

Ray froze.

The darkness thinned in front of him as a shape emerged: a man with a violin tucked beneath his chin, head tilted slightly to the side, eyes pale and unseeing yet smiling.

Ray stammered, "I… I didn't say that out loud, did I?"

"Oh yes," Jonas said cheerfully. "Very loud. Trembling with sincerity. Quite charming, really."

Ray blinked at him.

"You… you're blind."

Jonas grinned. "Goodness. Don't hold back, next you'll tell me I'm tall."

Ray's face flushed. "Sorry! I just meant…"

"No need to apologize," Jonas said, lowering his violin. "Sight is terribly overrated. People rely on it far too much. They miss all the important things, like… oh, for instance, the fact that you're absolutely terrified right now."

Ray swallowed. "Is it that obvious?"

Jonas tapped his violin bow lightly against Ray's chest, "Your heartbeat is doing the tango."

Ray winced. "Sorry."

"Don't apologize for being alive," Jonas replied. "It's one of your more endearing qualities."

Ray blinked fast. "Um… who are you?"

"Jonas," he said with a small bow. "Professional wanderer, part-time musician, occasional reality wrangler. And you, my large and trembling friend, are Ray."

Ray stiffened. "How did you…?"

Jonas smirked. "Let's just say your presence has been… announced."

Ray's shield gave a quiver.

Jonas leaned in. "Ah, yes. He likes you. Mystical armor are mysterious creatures. They have unusual taste."

Ray froze. "Mystical… what?!"

Jonas patted his shoulder but landed somewhere near Ray's collarbone.
"Not to worry. Probably."

"Probably?!" Ray stammered.

"Alright, ninety percent sure," Jonas said with a smirk.

"NINETY?!" Ray gasped.

Jonas raised his bow like a conductor calming an orchestra.

"Ray," he said gently, "I promise: the realm does not want to eat you. At least not today. Extremely messy business."

Ray stared at him. Then, despite everything, the fear, the darkness, the strange beads of sweat running down his spine, Ray snorted a laugh. Just a tiny one. Jonas smiled.

"There it is. Much better."

Ray rubbed the back of his neck. "Alright. So, where's the kid?"

"Simple," Jonas said, offering his hand. "You walk with me."

"Lead the way," Ray said, gesturing toward the passage ahead.

Jonas nodded approvingly. "Good lad. Let's go before something with too many teeth wakes up."

Ray steadied himself.

Jonas patted his hand. "Don't worry. I'll scream first."

Ray blinked. "…That doesn't help."

"It helps me." And with that, Jonas guided Ray deeper into the realm, violin humming softly in the darkness like a beacon of impossible comfort.

They walked for a moment in silence; the violin purred their only compass. Ray's breathing steadied, his pace matched Jonas's, the two of them moving in unison.

Then Ray hesitated. His steps slowed.

"Jonas," he whispered. "Why would you help me?"

Jonas didn't answer immediately. He simply continued walking, his pace unhurried, as if the question had been asked long ago and he'd been waiting all this time to answer it properly.

When he finally spoke, his voice was soft and knowing all at once.

"Because, Ray," he said, "you helped me long before you stepped inside this Door."

Ray frowned. The words made no sense. He'd never met Jonas before. He was certain of that.

"I don't understand," Ray said.

"You will," Jonas replied, tilting his head toward the unseen path ahead. "But not yet. Come now before the shadows remember they're hungry."

After a time, Ray couldn't say how long, the darkness began to gradually thin, like dawn breaking through fog. The violin's purr grew stronger, and ahead, light began to gather.

Jonas slowed his pace. Then stopped.

"Do you see it?" he asked softly.

Ray squinted into the dimness. "Yeah, ahead, the darkness had parted it looks like smoke clearing after a fire's been put out." Stone walls emerged from shadow, and beyond the chamber, vast openness.

"Good," Jonas touched his arm gently, his hand lingered for just a moment. "The path is clear from here. You'll find your way easily now."

Ray glanced at him. "You're heading out?"

"I need to prepare," Jonas said simply, but you won't be lost, Ray. The light will guide you. And the stones will welcome you."

Ray nodded slowly. He had walked into darker situations than this; he could handle a little magical darkness.

Jonas nodded, then with a small smile, turned and walked toward the shadow, his violin still humming, until the shadow swallowed him whole.

Ray took a breath, straightened his shoulders, and began to walk forward, one careful step at a time, toward the stone chamber and whatever waited beyond.

Chapter 19- The Stone Circle

The chamber lay at the heart of the Red Door, not the deepest place, but the one everything curved towards. A wide circle of standing stones rose from the floor like the ribs of something ancient and patient, each column etched with markings worn by time. Some glowed faintly. Some slept silently.

Jonas sat on a low slab near the center, violin resting across his knees, bow laid carefully beside it. He was not playing. He was listening.

The space hummed with layered resonance, not sound exactly, but with alignment. Threads that were tightening.

Footsteps approaching from different corridors, each carrying a different rhythm, a different weight. They were coming.

Jonas smiled to himself. “Take your time,” he murmured. “You’ve got a long way to go.”

- Claire.

Claire followed Kaelith through the garden’s warm glow, trying to reconcile the impossible beauty around her with the heaviness she’d carried for years. The air shimmered soft gold at her fingertips as they walked, but beneath the serenity, she felt a tug, a faint thread pulling her eastward without urgency, more like… recognition. Kaelith paused, sensing her drifting attention.

"You feel them, don't you?" He murmured.

Claire frowned. "Them?"

He lifted his gaze toward the distant corridor where the garden opened into darkness.

"The others. Children of the Weave. You were never meant to walk alone, Claire."

She shivered. "Why now?"

Kaelith offered a small, knowing smile. "Because the world beyond this door is unraveling and so are the ones in your world. This place calls you together for a reason."

Claire felt the pull again, stronger now, like a heartbeat calling to her as a memory.

In the distance, a flicker of silver light brightened in the corridor.

Claire drew a breath. "What's happening?"

"They are coming," Kaelith said gently. "And you must meet them."

He stepped back, fading into the garden light. "Go, Claire. Your path begins where theirs converges."

Claire hesitated for only a moment before she followed the silver glow into the corridor.

She entered quietly, exhaustion still present in her posture, but it no longer bent her spine. She paused just inside the ring of stones, one hand resting lightly over her heart, as if orienting herself by something newly steady.

Her gaze swept the chamber, lingering on the symbols, the breathing stillness of the space.

"It feels…" she searched for the word, "…held."

Jonas inclined his head. "It often does, for those who know how much they carry."

Claire startled slightly, then met his eyes.

"You know," she said.

"I listen," Jonas replied. "And sometimes, that's enough."

She didn't question him further. She stepped fully into the circle, the stone beneath her feet firm, unmoving as if it trusted her to stand there.

- Aaron

Aaron burst in next. His dragon trotted proudly alongside his leg as he wandered deeper into the realm, eyes wide, mouth parted in awe. Every doorway revealed something wondrous: drifting lights, floating glyphs, a chamber of spirals that moved whenever he blinked.

But then the dragon stiffened. A faint hum shivered beneath Aaron's feet, subtle, steady, magnetic.

"Do you feel that?" Aaron whispered.

The dragon chirped, nudging Aarons leg urgently before pointing its snout down a long, gently curving passage.

Aaron's pulse quickened.

"Should we go?"

The dragon nodded.

The pulsing beneath the floor matched the beat of Aaron's heartbeat. He did not know where he was being called to, but he knew it wasn't random.

Something was ahead. Something familiar. Something important.

He gathered his courage, tied the obsidian shard around his neck, and followed the dragon closely, running. He skidded to a stop just inside the large stone circle, eyes wide, breath quick, a grin threatening to break across his face despite himself.

“This place is amazing,” he breathed.

At his heels padded the small dragon, tail flicking, nose twitching as it took in the space. It chirped softly, then sneezed a harmless curl of smoke dissipating in the air.

Claire blinked. Then she laughed. A real laugh. Light, surprised, unmistakably human.

“Well,” she said. “That explains a few things.”

Aaron beamed, clearly relieved. “He’s friendly. Mostly.” The dragon puffed up proudly.

Jonas rose slowly from his seat, setting the violin aside. He crouched slightly, bringing himself closer to Aaron’s height. “You listened,” Jonas said. Aaron shrugged, suddenly shy. “I guess.”

The dragon stepped forward and nudged Aaron’s leg, then glanced up at Jonas with open curiosity. Jonas smiled. “Yes. You did.”

- Ray.

Ray entered the stone circle third. He moved carefully, shoulders broad, steps deliberate. The shield was held low at his side, as natural as his breathing.

His eyes scanned the garden out of habit, noting angles, distances, and exits.

Then he saw Aaron. Relief struck him hard enough to still his feet.

“You’re all right,” Ray said quietly. Aaron turned, confused. “Uh… yeah?”

Ray exhaled slowly. “Good.”

The dragon regarded Ray thoughtfully, then padded over and bumped its head against his shin.

Ray froze. Then, very carefully, relaxed.

“Guess that’s settled, nope, not surprised at all,” he murmured.

Claire watched him with new eyes without suspicion but with recognition. “You stand between things,” she said gently. Ray glanced at her, surprised.

“…Yeah,” he admitted. “I guess do.”

- Sage

Arrived last, or rather appeared. One moment, the space between two stones was empty, the next it wasn’t. Sage stood there as though the chamber had decided they belonged and adjusted accordingly.

Their gaze traced the symbols carved into the pillars, following lines only they seemed to notice. A faint smear of charcoal darkened one fingertip.

They stopped short when they took in the others. “Oh,” Sage said softly. “So this is where the line ends.”

Jonas smiled. “No,” he corrected. “It’s where it began to intersect.”

Sage nodded, satisfied. They stepped into the circle.

Chapter 20 – The journey begins

The stones pulsed faintly as they entered, five distinct rhythms finding alignment, like notes resolving into a chord.

Sage felt it before they saw it. A pull, gentle but insistent, drawing their attention to one of the standing stones. Their breath caught as their eyes found the symbol carved deep into the weathered surface: a flowing line, branching and curving like charcoal across paper. Like the Mark on their hand. Their fingers lifted, hovering just above the surface.

Ray's gaze swept the circle with a keen, practiced assessment. His eyes stopped on the stone opposite Sage's. A shield, broad and protective, etched with lines that suggested weight and endurance. He exhaled slowly, his hand moving unconsciously to rest against his side where his own shield hung. The carved symbol pulsed once, acknowledging him.

Claire drifted toward a third stone without deciding to, drawn by something she felt rather than saw. Two hands joined together, fingers interlaced, palms pressed close. The symbol glowed softly, warm as a heartbeat. She felt the ache in her chest ease slightly, as if something had recognized her.

Aaron's eyes caught on the stone to his left, an arrowhead, sharp and clean, pointing forward. Something in his chest tightened. He moved toward it, pulse quickening, unable to look away.

Jonas stepped to the center, his violin humming softly in his hands. Behind him, the fifth stone bore a symbol of echoing curves, waves of sound rippling outward, layered and infinite. He didn't need to see it to know it was there.

“None of you were summoned,” Jonas said plainly, his voice carrying through the chamber. “And none of you were chosen because you are exceptional.”

Aaron frowned, glancing away from the arrowhead. “Hey…”

Jonas held up a hand, smiling. “Exceptional isn’t the point. You are here because the Weave is breaking,” he continued. “Not tearing and not collapsing but breaking, unevenly, places slipping out of rhythm, it’s being destroyed.”

Sage inhaled sharply. “I’ve seen the fractures.”

“I know,” Jonas said.

Ray shifted his weight. “And us?”

“You each hold a way of seeing the world that cannot replace the others,” Jonas replied. “Alone, you would notice the damage. Together…”

He let the silence finish the thought.

Claire folded her arms loosely, “Together, we might help it and stop the destruction,” she said.

Jonas nodded once. “Exactly.”

The dragon chirped, as if in agreement.

The stones hummed softly. Somewhere deep within the Red Door, something aged and patient took notice.

The gathering was complete. Not because they were ready, but because they were finally aligned.

And beyond the chamber, the path forward waited, not yet revealed.

And the five symbols carved into the standing stones glowed brightly.

“Well,” said Jonas, smiling at all of them. “Shall we begin?”

Chapter 21 – The First Night

They set off along a winding path bordered by towering blue ferns and yellow crystal stones. The air grew cooler as they climbed. Birds made of drifting leaves scattered when the dragon chirped at them.

Sage trailed a hand along the stones as they walked. "Everything here feels loved," they said quietly.

Jonas nodded. "The weave is untouched here; this realm remembers its caretakers, even when the caretakers forget themselves."

Claire touched Sage's arm gently. "Where do you think this will lead?" Sage smiled, "I Wonder"

The fire was already burning when they reached the clearing. It sat at the center of a shallow stone bowl, burning low and steady, casting light that softened the edges of the world rather than sharpening them. The chamber opened upward here, the ceiling dissolving into a dark, starless expanse that felt more like sky than stone.

Jonas set down his violin case with a small sigh. "Well," he said lightly, "this seems hospitable."

Aaron stared. "Did the fire know we were coming?"

Jonas smiled. "It knows someone would need it."

They gathered slowly, uncertain of their places. Ray unrolled his bedroll where he could see every approach, settled in without fuss. Claire sat cross-legged near the fire, palms open toward the heat, shoulders loosening inch by inch. Sage lingered at the edge, watching how shadows bent and didn't quite behave.

The dragon curled near Aaron's knees as they sat against a boulder close to the fire, its tail wrapped neatly around itself, eyes bright.

For a while, no one spoke. The fire crackled. Stone shifted softly beneath them. Somewhere far away, the Red Door sealed and satisfied.

Claire broke the silence first "So," she said, voice tentative but honest, "does anyone else feel like… if they stop moving, everything might catch up to them?"

Ray huffed a quiet laugh. "That's one way to put it."

Sage nodded slowly. "Stillness reveals things. Sometimes more than motion does."

Aaron poked at the fire with a stick. "I think it's nice," he said. "It's like… camping. Except indoors sort of, and magical, and there's a dragon."

The dragon chirped in agreement.

Jonas chuckled. "Perspective is everything."

Ray glanced at Jonas. "Are you going to tell us where we're headed?"

"Soon," Jonas replied. "But not yet."

Sage tilted their head. "Are you waiting for something?"

Jonas met their gaze. "Someone."

The fire shifted, a little higher and a little brighter.

Sage stiffened. “Oh,” they murmured. “That’s not…”

The vision hit them like a charcoal splat across the mind.

Sage saw a vast sleeping shape of stone and earth, a mountain folded in on itself, breathing slow and deep, its pulse matching the rhythm of the fire.

They saw fractures, not wounds, but stress lines running through the land like cracked glaze.

A sound followed. Music, low, dissonant, and repetitive.

A rhythm out of step with the world.

Sage gasped and staggered forward, dropping to one knee feeling slightly disoriented.

Ray was at their side instantly, shield angled outward.

“You all right?”

Sage swallowed hard. “There’s something asleep, and somethings… wrong with the rhythm.”

Jonas’s expression sobered. “A giant,” he said quietly. “Dorma.”

Aaron’s eyes went wide. “Like…, like a real giant?”

“Yes, it is like a mountain that remembers how to walk,” Jonas replied.

Jonas turned toward Claire, his expression gentle but intent.

"Claire," he said quietly. "Put your hands on the ground."

She hesitated, glancing at the others. "What…”

"Steady your breathing," Jonas continued, his voice calm as a held note. "Feel what's beneath. Not just the earth, but what the earth is holding. Everything is energy, feel the energy of the earth, the rocks and Dorma."

Claire knelt slowly, pressing her palm flat against the cool stone. She closed her eyes, inhaling deeply, trying to quiet the rush of her own pulse.

At first, there was nothing.

Then --

A weight. Vast and ancient. A deep, strained breath that seemed to come from miles below.

Her chest tightened with a sensation that wasn't hers. “I can feel a buzzing, a sensation that feels weary. It's Laden,” she whispered, eyes still closed. “It’s hurting,” she said. “Not angry. Just… weary and concerned.”

The fire crackled sharply.

Jonas lifted his violin, resting it against his shoulder but not yet playing.

“When Dorma stirs,” he said, “the land shifts. Some paths open, others close.”

Sage shook their head. “The rhythm is wrong. If it wakes like that…”

“It won’t wake cleanly,” Jonas finished.

Silence settled, heavier now.

Aaron looked down at the dragon, who gazed back up at him, unafraid.

“So,” Aaron said slowly, “we’re supposed to… help it?”

Jonas smiled, a broad smile, one of pride. “Yes,” he said. “That’s exactly it.”

Ray stood, shield steady at his side. “Then we should move before it wakes on its own. Not to rush,” he said. “But we must move.”

Claire rose as well, surprising herself with how much lighter she felt.

Jonas nodded. “Rest first. Even the Weave pauses before a long journey. This journey will test both your body and your spirit.” he said.

The fire settled back into itself, flames lowering, steady once more.

They slept there, not deeply, but together.

And somewhere beneath stone and memory, the giant dreamed of music it could no longer hear.

Chapter 22 - Dorma

The path had been easy and straight; they reached Dorma as the land began to pulse unevenly, a definite change, as the light began to dim.

The giant lay like a gigantic granite mountain; time had weathered the rocks and added well-worn groves and crevices. Moss and lichen bloomed across its surface in muted greens and greys. Hardy shrubs clustered in the hollows, their roots burrowing deep, holding the ancient stone together as much as they were held by it.

They entered a cave where the ground sloped downward, stone giving way to packed earth, roots threading through the walls like veins. With every step, the vibration beneath their feet grew more pronounced and strained, as though something immense was holding itself still.

Claire sensed it first. An awareness blooming in her chest; they were not alone here. Something sensed her as much as she sensed it.

"Something's awake," she whispered. "But it's afraid to move."

Jonas nodded. "Dorma has slept through many changes and for many centuries. Waking now… costs something."

They emerged into a vast hollow where the ceiling vanished into darkness. The ground beneath them curved gently upward and downward, forming the unmistakable rise and fall of a chest.

Stalactites and stalagmites adorned the cave and gave off a vibrating echo with every word spoken.

Stone and crystals shaped into shoulders and spine. Soil pressed into muscle and sinew. Dorma was not inside the mountain. Dorma was the mountain.

Aaron swallowed. “Whoa… how is that possible?”

Sage stepped forward, eyes tracing the air inside the giant's form. Lines appeared in their vision, silver threads woven through stone and earth, connecting breath to bedrock. But the pattern was wrong. The threads pulled taut in some places, slack in others, the whole structure straining like a frayed rope held at breaking point, kept together by only a few remaining strands strained and tangled. They looped back on themselves, crossing and recrossing as a necklace chain snarled in a drawer. Some paths led forward, others circled back, and others just seemed to echo, repeating the same route, twice, three times, layering over each other until it was impossible to tell which was real. It’s confused." Sage breathed. "The paths are all knotted together."

Jonas lifted his violin slowly, his expression intent. He played a soft questioning note and seemed to listen to an answer only he could hear. “Dorma remembers every path it’s ever helped,” he said quietly. “But the weave breaking has tangled them. It can’t tell which way leads forward anymore.

He raised his bow, “So… we help it remember”. He did not play a melody that would wake a memory.

A low, patient note held long enough for the rock to feel the vibration, followed by silence. He waited, head tilted and listened. Jonas played again, a different note this time, higher, clearer. He let it ring out, then fade. The reverberation shifted slightly.

Dorma’s breath caught. Then, slowly, released.

“There,” Jonas murmured. "That one's still alive.”

He drew the bow across the strings again, this time playing two notes in sequence, the second following the first like a path unfolding. The sound resonated through the chamber, and one of the silver threads in Sage's vision brightened.

“I see it,” Sage whispered. “That thread… It's separating from the others.”

Jonas nodded, eyes closed, violin bow moving with careful precision. He played the sequence again, then added a third note. The melody was simple, almost childlike, but each note seemed to pull gently at the tangled threads, coaxing them apart without forcing.

Another thread brightened. Then another.

The ground beneath them rolled gently, not enough to unbalance, but enough to be felt. Dust drifted from the ceiling like falling pollen.

Claire knelt, pressing her hands to the ground as Jonas had taught her. She could feel it now, Dorma's confusion easing, just slightly, as the paths began to separate in its ancient memory.

“It's working,” she said softly.

Jonas continued, his music patient and unhurried. Some notes he repeated, others he let fade into silence, waiting to see if the land would answer. Slowly, carefully, he traced the true path with sound, distinguishing it from the echoes and loops that had snarled around it.

Ray watched, shield resting against his leg, his expression thoughtful. Aaron stood beside him, the dragon sat by his feet, both utterly still, and amazed.

This was how it was done. Not with force and not with haste. But with listening and sensing.

Jonas played one final sequence, four notes, rising and falling like breath. The sound hung in the air, clear and certain.

The ground beneath them rolled again. Dorma's breath released.

The stone wall ahead of them softened, then split along a natural seam. Roots drew back. Earth parted. A passage opened. Dorma had remembered.

Jonas lowered the violin, his shoulders easing. “That's the way forward,” he said quietly.

Aaron frowned. “How do you know?”

Jonas smiled faintly. “The old mountain and I have always understood each other. It was waiting to hear my voice before it would trust anyone with its secret paths. The Weave has made everything confused, but when Dorma heard the music, it remembered.”

The giant slowly turned, leaned, and in that shift, the path aligned, pointing outward, toward a place where the air beyond carried a sharp, bitter edge.

Sage stiffened. “That forest…”

They could feel it now, a presence bristling just beyond the threshold. Growth without balance. Life turned inward and defensive.

“Something’s wrong with it,” Sage said.

“It’s been tainted,” Jonas said

“I think I can feel its pain,” Claire added quietly.

Ray adjusted his grip on the shield, stepping closer to Aaron without thinking.

The dragon lifted its head, wings twitching uneasily, and it stayed close to Aaron, eyes alert.

Dorma groaned, its presence pressed gently against all of them as if in agreement.

“This is where the land breaks. This is where it must be met gently.” Jonas stated.

The passage opened fully. A wind rushed through, carrying the smell of sap, thick, bitter, and toxic. Thorns scraped against stone somewhere beyond.

Jonas exhaled. “The Bramble Forest.”

Aaron glanced back once, at the rise and fall of the mountain behind them.

“Will Dorma be okay?” he asked with concern.

Jonas placed a hand on Aaron’s shoulder. “Yes,” he said gently. “If we mend the Weave, Dorma will heal with it.”

They turned and stepped out onto the path together. Ahead, the forest waited.

Chapter 23- The Bramble Forest

The forest announced itself before they crossed its threshold.

The air changed first, thickened, sharp with the smell of sap and rot. Then the light dimmed, as if something had drawn a curtain overhead. Branches interlaced high above them, their twisted, gnarly looking limbs blocking out the sky in uneven patches.

Thorns scraped stones with intent, like butchers sharpening their knives

Sage slowed, eyes tracing lines only they could see. "This place doesn't want us moving straight through, but that's the way the lines flow."

Ray stepped half a pace forward, shield angled slightly outward. "Feels like it's testing us."

Jonas tilted his head, listening. "No," he said quietly. "It's terrified."

They took only a few steps before the forest reacted.

Vines slithered across the path, thick as ropes, their surfaces studded with barbs that glistened with dark, dripping acidic sap. Branches bent inward, creaking under their own tension, narrowing the space until it felt like the forest was breathing down on them.

Aaron felt it in his chest, tightening, like the moment before getting called out in class.

"This place hates us," he whispered.

A vine lashed out. Ray raised the shield just in time; the impact rang when it struck the metal. The vine recoiled, sap hissing where it splattered against the ground.

"Careful," Jonas warned. "Force will only teach it to be crueler."

The path split abruptly, tearing into two, Jagged and treacherous.

Sage stopped short. "The lines diverge here."

Before anyone could respond, the ground shifted beneath Aaron's feet.

He stumbled forward, catching himself and then realized the others were no longer directly behind him. They were on the other side of the deep divide.

"Hey…?" he called.

The sound of his voice was swallowed almost instantly.

"Aaron?" Claire turned sharply.

The forest moved. Branches slid together, snapping and closing. The path between them folded in on itself, replaced by a wall of thorns.

"Aaron!" Ray surged forward, shield raised.

Jonas caught his arm. "Wait."

Ray bristled. "But he is only a kid."

"And the forest knows that" Jonas said grimly.

Aaron ran forward blindly and instinctively.

The path ahead opened where the one behind him closed, roots shifting just enough to allow him through. His heart hammered, breath sharp in his ears. "This is stupid," he muttered. "This is really stupid." The dragon stayed close, wings tucked tight, steady at Aaron's side.

The forest hissed. *"You are too small, and too slow, you are always behind."*

Aaron skidded to a stop behind a large stump, hands shaking.

"No," he said aloud. "That's not true."

A shadow moved between the trees.

Something watching. Something lurking.

Aaron took a shaky breath and crawled forward into a small opening in the stump, scraping his knee. Dragon moved directly behind him and followed closely.

The opening led into a tunnel that twisted and turned. It opened slightly, then narrowed again. Dirt crumbled beneath his palms. Roots touched his head as he crawled. More than once, he froze, convinced the roots were moving closer.

Time stretched. He didn't know how long he had crawled. At last, the tunnel sloped upward, light bleeding in through a thin seam ahead. Aaron pushed harder until he burst through and tumbled into a small clearing.

He was on the other side of the brambles.

The forest loomed thick and snarled behind him, thorns interlocked like clenched teeth. Beyond them, he could hear voices, distant and muffled.

"Aaron!" Claire called.

"I'm here!" he shouted back, voice breaking with relief.

The hissing changed. Lower., watchful…

Claire stood before the wall of thorns, chest tight, hands trembling.

She could hear it now. The forest wasn't just hissing. It was groaning; it reminded her of when her patients were groaning in pain. A deep, aching sound threaded through the roots and tree bark, as if the land itself were under strain.

Sage pressed their palms to their temples. "It's tangled, terrified. Everything's growing in the wrong direction."

Ray clenched his jaw. "Tell me how to break through."

Jonas shook his head. "We don't break this."

Claire stepped forward. She didn't raise her voice. She reached out. Her fingers brushed the vine.

The forest recoiled, violently, thorns snapping outward. Bubbles of sap erupted thick and tacky, blackening where they burst, smoking with a sour stench.

Claire didn't pull back. She closed her eyes, took a deep breath, and listened. "Oh," she breathed.

Everyone froze.

"No," Claire said gently. "It's in pain and hurt things lash out and to hurt others," Claire said softly.

The words weren't an explanation. They were recognized. She pressed her palm fully to the bark. "You've been holding too much," she murmured. "It's okay, you don't have to keep everyone out."

The groaning deepened, then softened. Sap dulled, losing its sharp sheen. Thorns loosened their grip. The whispering slowed, threads of sound untangling into something closer to breath.

A narrow opening appeared.

Ray exhaled. “Over there.”

They moved through carefully, stepping over and around sharp, threatening thorns and brambles.

On the other side, Aaron ran straight into Claire’s arms, wrapping around her as she caught him tight. “You found your way,” she said, voice steady though her hands shook.

Aaron nodded, pressing his face into her shoulder. “It was loud, and dark, and… really scary.” She held him for a moment longer.

The forest settled behind them, not healed, but no longer lashing out.

They moved on together, the whispering fading into uneasy silence, and deeper within the distortion, something was listening.

Chapter 24- The Salt Cove

They didn't speak for a long time.

The forest thinned gradually, its twisted branches loosening their grip as the land sloped upward. The air was cool and damp, with the faint scent of salt. The whispering faded behind them, replaced by something broader, deeper. The sound of water.

They emerged onto a narrow ledge carved into the side of a cliff where stone gave way to air.

Below them, the land dropped away in layered shelves of black volcanic rock, each one worn smooth by time and tide, the cove curved inward like a cupped hand.

It should have been beautiful. And once, it had been.

The water shimmered under a thin wash of sunlight, but the reflection cracked as it moved. Dark seams ran through the surface, not as waves or shadows, but lines where the sea seemed to hesitate; it moved as if covered by a thick, hard oil slick, unsure how to continue.

Jonas stopped walking. He didn't speak at first. His head tilted slightly, as if listening to something layered beneath it.

"I know this place," he said quietly.

The others turned toward him.

"I've stood here before," Jonas continued. "Long ago, the water used to sing back then. Soft. And playful. You could hear the cliffs' answer if you played the right note."

He smiled faintly with recognition.

"It was one of the few places where the Weave rested easily."

Ray looked out over the cove, brow furrowed. "It doesn't look very rested now."

"No," Jonas said. "The Weave has stolen its beauty and locked it deep. What's left is just the shape of what it used to be."

The dragon crouched near the edge, tail flicking once, unease humming through its small frame.

Sage had already moved closer to the cliff.

They knelt, fingers tracing the stone without touching it at first. Their eyes unfocused, tracking something invisible as charcoal lines flickered through their mind, waiting.

"The lines don't cross here," Sage said slowly. "They slide, that's why the water can't decide which way to move."

Jonas nodded. "The rhythm's broken sideways."

Sage reached into their satchel and withdrew a stub of charcoal, well-used, edges softened by time.

Ray frowned. "You're going to draw… on rock?"

Sage didn't look up. "I'm not drawing on it."

They leaned forward and let the charcoal come in contact with the stone.

The line appeared, dark, clean, deliberate, following the natural grain of the rock as if it had always been there. Sage's hand moved steadily, confident, sketching a thin path that curved downward along the cliff face.

As the line formed, the water below responded. The dark seams shifted subtly, pulling toward the line's direction, as if the sea were remembering which way it used to flow.

Ray watched, his expression intent. "You're not fixing it."

"No," Sage replied softly. "Just giving it a suggestion."

The path completed itself not as a bridge or stairs but as a visual guide, a gentle directive etched into the stone.

The water created a small wake and then steadied slightly.

Ray exhaled. "So that's what you do."

Sage stood, hands smudged black. "That's what I remember doing."

"The cove will hold," Jonas said. "For now," he smiled this time, with warmth edged by relief.

Ray looked back at the path they had traveled, forest, mountain, and the brambles. He shook his head slowly. "You know, when I woke up yesterday, I thought the weirdest part of my day would be finding a half-eaten birthday cake in a recycling bin." He gestured at the cove, the dragon, the charcoal line on ancient stone. "Turns out I was wrong."

Aaron snorted despite himself.

Claire watched quietly from a few steps back, sensing the shift without stepping into it. This wasn't her moment to lead.

A breeze swept across the cliff, carrying the sound of water splashing unevenly, but no longer struggling.

Jonas stood still for a long moment, head tilted, listening to something beneath the wind. His expression shifted with nostalgia.

“The lines keep going,” Sage said quietly, following his gaze. “Away from the water.”

Jonas nodded slowly. “Into the hills, the Weave is tighter there, older, more tangled.” He paused, weighing his next words. “What we've faced so far has been the edges of the breaking fragments. But ahead…Ahead, we're walking toward the center.”

Aaron swallowed. “Into what?”

Jonas pointed toward the land beyond the forest, where the air thickened and the light bent oddly.

“Into the hills,” he said. “And beyond them… worse.”

The cove shimmered below them. Ahead, the Weave tightened, and the path was recalled, chosen, waiting.

Chapter 25- Echo hunters

They made camp above the cove as night settled in.

No full fire this time, just a low ember cupped in stone, barely enough to give shape to their shadows. The sea below reflected moonlight unevenly, its cracked surface catching silver in broken slashes. The air was cold and anxious.

They slept lightly, wrapped in cloaks and borrowed warmth, each drifting only partway into rest.

The dragon did not sleep at all. It stirred first a subtle shift of weight, claws scraping dirt. Its head lifted, nostrils flaring. A low, uneasy sound vibrated deep in its chest.

Aaron's eyes snapped open. "What is it?" he whispered.

The dragon's pupils had narrowed to slits. Its wings tucked closer to its body as it sniffed the air once, twice, then recoiled slightly.

A smell drifted on the breeze. It smelled rancid. Something ominous.

Ray sat up, hand already closing around the shield. "Anyone else smell that?"

Sagc nodded slowly. "Yes. It's… wrong."

Jonas was on his feet now, head tilted, listening intently. His expression had hardened, the faint humor gone. “I think we are being followed,” he said.

Claire’s stomach tightened. “By who?”

Jonas didn’t answer immediately. He hadn’t heard them this soon before.

Below them, the cove darkened further as clouds passed over the moon; the light itself was being absorbed. The water stilled unnaturally, waves freezing mid-motion.

The dragon hissed softly. From the edge of the forest, something moved.

Gliding, making use of the darkness to stay hidden.

A shape separated itself from the shadows between the trees. Tall, thin, indistinct, its edges blurring like smoke, another followed and then another.

They did not approach the camp directly. They circled like a pride of hungry animals.

A foul scent thickened, metallic and bitter, as rotting flesh mixed with damp earth. Aaron gagged, covering his mouth.

“They don’t like the living creatures,” Sage whispered. “Or any that I drew.”

“They’re wary,” Jonas agreed. “Not afraid.”

The shapes paused at the edge of the clearing, their presence pressing inward like pressure against glass.

No eyes were visible. But they were looking.

Claire hugged her knees, breath shallow. She could feel it now, the weight of despair radiating from them, heavy and invasive, pressing against old griefs, old fears.

Ray stepped slightly in front of Aaron, shield angled outward. "If they attack…"

"They won't," Jonas said quietly. "They'll just keep watch for now."

The dragon let out a low warning growl, flame flickering briefly behind its teeth.

The shapes recoiled just a fraction, just enough.

Jonas lifted his violin and drew a single, steady note that vibrated through the stone beneath their feet. The sound was thin. But true.

The darkness hesitated. The shapes wavered, edges fraying like mist caught in the wind. One retreated back into the trees, another lingered, then followed.

The smell faded slowly.

Aaron let out the breath he'd been holding. "What… were those things?"

Jonas lowered the violin. "Echo-hunters, or some call them the Shadow Mew, because they hang out in the shadows. They track fractures, fear, and unfinished grief; they are the messengers of the one controlling all this destruction."

Sage swallowed. "So, they'll keep coming."

"Yes," Jonas said. "As long as the Weave keeps tearing."

Silence settled again, thinner now, brittle.

The dragon finally relaxed slightly, curling close to Aaron once more, eyes still open.

No one slept at all after that.

And far beyond the cove, the darkness adjusted its course.

Patient, waiting. Learning their scent.

Chapter 26 - Through the Echoes

The hills did not let them pass all at once. They narrowed and slowed them instead.

“So, this is where it happens,” he said quietly.

Ray frowned. “Where what happens?”

“Where the land stops asking politely.”

Jonas turned slowly, facing each of them in turn. “We don't outrun this,” he said. “And we don't fight it. These hills reflect what we carry. If we don't face it, we stay here.”

Aaron swallowed. “Face… what, exactly?”

Jonas's voice softened. “The part of yourself, the echoes already know.”

The wind surged, and the hills answered.

Aaron heard children's voices. Familiar. Sharp-edged.

“You don’t belong.”
“Something’s wrong with you.”
“You made it all up.”

“That’s right, run away.”

“I didn't do anything wrong,” Aaron whispered.

His chest tightened. He took a step back, heart hammering.

The dragon pressed closer, warmth steady against Aaron's leg.

He folded his fingers around the dragon glass around his neck. “I am brave… I am brave.”

Aaron crouched, hands clenched in the dirt. His voice shook, but he spoke anyway.

“I’m not running,” he said. “I’m right here.”

The laughter faltered.

Not gone.

Ray's echo came differently.

The hill before him shuddered, its slopes easing just slightly

No voices, just looks. Ray's jaw tightened. He heard his own thoughts…

“Too big, must be dangerous, better to cross the street, bigfoot.”

Glances sliding away. Shoulders turning. The space people left between themselves and him, being remembered, reinforced. “I've spent my whole life making sure no one gets hurt,” he said aloud. “Even when they thought I wouldn’t.”

He lifted the shield, not defensively, but as a weight as proof.

Sage's echo was visual. The wind shifted direction.

“You’re not enough, you don’t belong, you're weird, get a real job.”

Sage's hands trembled.

“I remember,” Sage said quietly. “Even when I forget why, I know my purpose.”

They lifted the charcoal and drew a single line, imperfect, doubled, and slightly curved.

The looping hills shuddered, a path beginning to form, faint and unstable, but present.

Claire stood very still.

Patient’s voices, she knew well, the sound of the patient’s family members crying, mourning their loss.

“You are an imposter, you can’t help anyone, you are alone, no one cares about you.”

Her breath caught, and a tear rolled down her cheek.

Jonas stepped closer, just being present, holding space.

Her breath caught. “I can help, and I do,” she said softly. “I am not alone. I did what I could. I loved, and I cared.”

Claire placed her palm on her chest, grounding herself.

The ache loosened. The air warmed slightly, and the hills groaned in resistance.

Still, something pushed back.

“That's not the hills,” Jonas said sharply. “That's interference.”

The air changed, shifted, colder now, icy finger tendrils weaving their way through fabric and up spines.

Sage's line wavered.

Ray stepped forward instinctively, shield raised this time defiantly.

The dragon growled, smoke strands trailing off in the wind.

From the far slope, a shadow pooled, not forming fully, not advancing, just watching.

The Shadow Maw.

The echoes twisted, overlapping unnaturally, bending toward despair rather than release.

Jonas lifted his violin and played a tune, steady and beautiful.

Softly, defiant and true.

A tune of memory and a tune of truth.

“Stand together,” he said firmly. “Don't pull away.”

The wind and the voices calmed, and the shadows subsided.

The path Sage had drawn, strengthened, extending forward, jagged and uneasy as the shadows receded.

Jonas exhaled slowly. “That was a test.”

Aaron bent and hugged the dragon. “I hate tests.”

Jonas smiled faintly. “You passed.”

They moved on, the hills finally allowing passage. Behind them, the echoes faded into uneasy silence.

Ahead, the land steepened. And somewhere beyond the next rise, something waited …to oppose them.

Chapter 27- The Shadow Maw

The attack came without sound. No warning cry and no rush of air.

Just a sudden absence as if the light around Aaron had been swallowed.

The dragon reacted first. It surged forward, a violent pulse of heat and motion, wings flaring instinctively as Aaron stumbled backward. The air thickened, pressing in, the smell hitting a heartbeat later, Cold iron, wet stone, and something rotten and starving.

The Shadow Maw unfolded itself from the hill's shadow.

It stretched tall, elongated, its edges unraveling and reforming as it moved. Where it passed, the ground dimmed, color draining as if memory itself were being consumed.

Aaron froze, unable to scream.

The Shadow Maw leaned closer, its presence crushing, suffocating. No mouth, but it felt hungry, vast, and focused.

The ground behind Aaron shuddered.

A fissure split the stone near Ray's feet, widening rapidly, the hill itself buckling under the Shadow Maw's pull.

"Ray!" Sage shouted

Ray stumbled and began to slip, shield scraping stone as the ground gave way beneath him.

Without thinking, Aaron moved. He didn't shout. He didn't look back. He ran straight toward Ray, standing on the other side, cleaning the fissure with a jump.

"Aaron, no!" Claire cried.

Aaron skidded on loose gravel, grabbed Ray's arm with both hands, and pulled, his small weight useless against the slope, but his grip fierce.

"Don't let go!" Aaron yelled, voice cracking.

Ray's eyes widened not with fear for himself but for the boy bracing against the collapsing ground.

"Aaron, get back!" "I'm too heavy."

"I've got you!" Aaron shouted, even as tears streaked down his face. "I've got you!"

The fissure widened some more. The Shadow Maw shifted its attention.

The hunger reoriented towards Aaron's fear and his defiance.

The dragon roared. This was not a warning. This was pure fury.

The sound was far bigger than the little dragon should make; it tore through the hills like thunder, ripping the sky apart.

The sound startled the shadow mew enough to release the grip on Ray. He collapsed backward onto protruding solid stone, breathing hard.

Aaron fell with him, landing on the stones, sobbing, hands still clenched in Ray's coat. At that moment, the dragon started to grow; it grew larger and larger. Wings unfurled wider than the path behind them. Scales caught the light and shone like copper on fire, no longer small, no longer contained. Gigantic claws spread out. Heat and flames rolled outward in waves, forcing the Shadow Maw to recoil. The dragon took flight, causing its own massive shadow to be cast over the travelers. It swooped and dived, searching, looking for something to sink its teeth into.

The Shadow Maw recoiled violently, shrieking in panic and shock.

The dragon landed and stood over them, vast and radiant, a living wall of flame and scale. Its roar came again, deeper this time, shaking the land itself.

The Shadow Maw retreated, dissolving into shadow, their presence tearing backward into the fractures from where they had emerged.

Before it vanished, its attention lingered on Aaron. Taking one last look in insolence.

Aaron pushed himself upright, wiping his face with his sleeve.

"I didn't think," he said, voice small. "I just…. I didn't want him to fall."

Ray sat up slowly, staring at Aaron as if seeing him for the first time.

"You pulled me back," Ray said quietly. "You shouldn't have been able to."

Aaron shrugged weakly. "I didn't do it alone."

The Shadow Maw now dissipated into shadow and silence. The hills were stilled.

The dragon stood in front of Aaron, head bowed, yellow eyes fixed on the boy. Aaron moved forward slowly, reaching out with a shaking hand to touch the dragon's snout. The dragon nuzzled into the palm of his hand as if to reassure Aaron, and it then began to shrink back, settling down beside him, head lowered, eyes still blazing with restrained fury.

Aaron stared. "You…" His voice broke. "You were… small."

The dragon huffed a warm rumbling sound, pressing its forehead gently into Aaron's Palm.

Jonas stepped forward.

His expression was not one of surprise; it was solemn.

"Well," he said quietly, "that settles it."

Ray glanced between Aaron and the dragon. "Settles what?"

Jonas knelt so he was eye level with Aaron.

"You weren't chosen because you're fearless," Jonas said. "Or because you're ready."

Aaron swallowed hard. "Then why?"

Jonas placed a steady hand over Aaron's heart.

"Because the Weave recognizes you as the boy king that you are, and it has great things in store for you."

He glanced at the dragon, which lowered its head further.

"Dragon guardians don't bond to power," Jonas continued. "They bond to calm inner strength and courage."

Claire stepped closer, voice gentle but certain. "And that's exactly what you showed when someone was in trouble, you showed courage and inner strength," she said.

Sage nodded slowly, eyes bright with something like respect. "The old stories always say the same thing."

Aaron's chest felt too tight. "I'm just a boy; I'm not a king. I don't want to be strong and brave," he whispered.

Jonas smiled softly, almost sad.

"Neither did the best ones. You'll be ready when the time comes. It's your destiny."

The dragon straightened, shuffling its wings with deliberate grace.

The hills exhaled. The Weave shuddered in acknowledgment.

And far away, something shifted its attention fully onto them.

Chapter 28- The Path of Broken Stones

The hills thinned as they climbed. Grass gave way to stone, then to long shelves of fractured rock that rose like frozen waves. The air grew thinner, sharper, carrying the scent of dust and something mineral, something archaic and unsettled.

Ahead, the path narrowed, becoming a pass that cut through the mountain's shoulder, its walls ragged and uneven, as if the stone itself had split under pressure rather than having been pushed up from the inner earth. Boulders lay scattered at odd angles, some balanced impossibly atop one another.

Sage stopped at the edge of it. "This place broke suddenly," they said. "Not naturally."

Jonas nodded. "When Dorma stretched, the land paid for it here."

Ray shifted the shield on his arm. "Looks like a bad place to linger."

Aaron stared up at the towering stone, the weight of it pressing down on him. He felt small again, yet more awarc.

The dragon crept ahead a few steps, sniffing the air, then paused, tail twitching once.

"It doesn't like this," Aaron said quietly.

"It shouldn't," Jonas replied. "The mountain tore itself open here. Stones don't forget that kind of stress."

They entered the pass carefully, and the sound changed immediately.

Footsteps reverberated too loudly, bouncing back at them from odd angles. The wind threaded through cracks in the rock, producing low, uneven tones that whistled eerie tunes.

Claire winced. "This place is loud."

They had gone only a short distance when the ground shifted beneath them like a tremor, just enough to send pebbles skittering down the slope behind.

Ray froze. "No one move."

Aaron stopped breathing.

A boulder ahead of them trembled, grinding softly against the rock beneath it.

Sage crouched, palm pressed to the ground. "The pressure's uneven. The path wants to collapse inward."

Jonas closed his eyes briefly, listening. "There's another way," he said. "But it's not obvious."

All eyes turned instinctively toward Aaron. He stiffened immediately. "I don't… I don't know what to do."

Jonas raised a hand gently. "No one's asking you to."

The relief was immediate and telling.

Sage rose slowly, gaze scanning the stone. "The fractures run diagonally," they said. "If we keep following the center, it'll give."

Ray frowned. "So, we hug the edge?"

Sage shook their head. "Too brittle."

They looked at Aaron again, this time expectantly.

"What does it feel like to you?" Sage asked.

Aaron swallowed, heart racing. He didn't want to be wrong.

He closed his eyes and took a deep breath, calming his nerves as he had seen Claire do many times.

The ground shuddered faintly and steadily beneath his feet. Like the way the floor vibrated when a train passed far below the city.

"Over there," he said hesitantly, pointing to a narrow ledge partway up the pass wall. "It feels… It's quieter."

Jonas smiled slightly. "That'll do."

They climbed carefully, moving in a single file. The ledge was narrow but solid, the stone less fractured than it looked. Below them, the central path shuddered and gave way, stones tumbling into the valley below.

Ray exhaled sharply. "Good call, kid."

Aaron flushed. "I don't know how I knew that…"

"You listened," Claire said gently. "That's enough."

They reached the far side of the pass and paused, looking back at the broken stone pathway now settling into uneasy stillness.

The dragon chirped softly, brushing against Aaron's leg.

Ahead, the land sloped downward again, not toward water this time, but toward a wide basin where mist gathered low and thick.

Jonas's expression tightened. "That's not fog," he said.

"What is it?" Aaron asked.

Jonas listened, frowning. "Memories," he said. "The kind that don't want to be remembered."

The pass of broken stone lay behind them. The Shadow Maw lay somewhere beyond sight.

And ahead, the mist waited heavily, full of things beyond time and space.

Chapter 29- The Basin of Lost Souls

The basin appeared just over the hill. It revealed itself only after the path gave up pretending to be a path at all when stone cut across a dead plains, the land collapsed into the memory of a river now dry as an old bone.
The ground was split into a thousand interlocking plates, each edged in pale dust, like broken pottery scattered by some ancient hand.
Black fissures veined the earth in every direction, deep enough to drink the light, as if the world had once been fluid here and something had commanded it to harden. Fine pale dust. Shrubs that had dried out and become golden brown tumbleweeds. The air grew unnervingly still, not a breath.

They felt it before they saw it, like pressure behind the eyes. A subtle pulling, like memory tugging at loose threads.

And the basin that lay below them was wide and shallow, carved into the earth as though a vast meteor had once pressed down and then risen again, leaving its absence behind. Its surface was smooth stone, veined with faint fractures that glimmered like frost beneath moonlight, though there was no moon here, no sky, either. Only a dim, pearlescent glow seemed to emanate from the basin itself.

As they drew closer, they saw names had been etched into the stone. Thousands of them.

Some sharp and deep, others worn thin by time or by forgetting. They spiraled inward from the rim, circling toward the basin's center where the stone darkened, as if soaked by something unseen. A staircase was carved into the outer rim descending, towards the center.

"What is this place?" Claire whispered.

Jonas did not answer at first. Sage had already stepped forward onto the first wrang, hand hovering just above the stone, fingers trembling. The moment they touched it, the basin reacted.

The names shifted. Yet the surface did not move, something changed in how they were perceived. Letters rearranged themselves in the mind. Strange sounds resounded without a source.

A voice rose as a whisper, it, wasn't loud or commanding, it was soft and intimate.

"Names are anchors", it said. "And anchors should be cut free."

Aaron staggered back, clutching his head. "I think…I remember things," he said. "Things that didn't happen to me."

Ray knelt at the edge of the basin, staring at a name etched near his knee. His breath caught.

"That was my wife's name," he said. "But no one here should know it."

Jonas said nothing. He was looking out at the basin's center, as if he could see it, to where the names were most eroded, scratched over, crossed out, sometimes replaced entirely. "I can feel the vibrations of each name; they each resonate differently like individual chords, these aren't just forgotten," he said finally. "Lost souls gather here. Souls that were lost in life, and don't know where to go in death."

Claire stepped down, off the final step, her hand brushing the wall for balance. The moment her boot touched the basin floor, the weight settled on her shoulders with absolute gravity. A thousand unfinished sentences were pressed against her chest.

They sensed her. They always did. At first, they appeared as silhouettes, soft ghost-like apparitions flickering at the edges of her vision. No faces, no names. Just the chance of wanting to be known again. Wanting to be remembered. Wanting to belong.

Claire closed her eyes. "Breathe", she reminded herself. "You can't help them all at once."

That was the mistake she had made before.

One name drifted like smoke closer than the rest. It shimmered weakly, its edges crumbling like wet paper. "I don't remember my name," it whispered. The voice was not sound, it was a thought.

Claire knelt. "That's all right," she said gently. "I will listen."

She placed her palm against the stone wall. The basin responded, veins of dim light pulsing outward in slow rings. This place had been made for her kind long before anyone remembered why.

"What do you remember?" Claire asked. The soul flickered. "Someone was waiting for me." The voice replied.

Pain bloomed behind Claire's eyes.

The fragments always came like this, incomplete, jagged, cruel in their simplicity.

She focused inward, on the quiet place she guarded fiercely. The place that lets her hold memory without drowning in it. She touched the soul with that inner hand.

And the story poured in. A man, or a woman, it no longer mattered. A life spent postponing joy. Letters never sent, apologies rehearsed but never spoken. A final moment of clarity arriving exactly one breath too late.

Claire gasped.

She felt the end as if it were her own, the sharp regret, the sudden understanding, the unbearable wish for more time for one more ordinary day.

Her knees hit the stone. This was the cost. She gathered the memory gently, compressing it into something survivable. Then she spoke the words that mattered most.

"You were seen," Claire said. "You were loved more than you knew, and you are not forgotten."

The soul stilled, just for a moment, and it became solid, clearer than it had ever been. A face emerged, blurred, but peaceful.

"Thank you," it said.

Then it dissolved into light and vanished upward through cracks in the sky that looked like a ceiling, a portal that led somewhere kinder.

Claire stayed kneeling, breath ragged.

One was never just one. They came faster now, sensing the opening, the permission.

A child who had waited too long at a bus stop, the bus never came, so they crossed the busy road.
A woman who died believing she had ruined everything. A man who clutched a promise he never got to keep. A young girl taken too soon by someone's bad intentions.

Each one took something from her. Not just inner strength, but something worse. The sacred space inside. Her chest felt too small to contain all this grief and still remain herself.

She pressed her forehead to the stone. “I can’t hold all of you,” she whispered. “Please.”

The basin answered with silence. Then footsteps….

Claire looked up sharply. No souls moved like that.

A figure stood a few steps up on the staircase, half in shadow, watching, not intruding.

“You should stop,” the figure said calmly.

Claire laughed weakly. “That’s what they all say.”

“Everything dies,” the figure replied. That got her attention.

“Who are you?” she asked.

“A witness, nothing more,” the figure said.

Claire pushed herself to her feet, swaying. The basin felt heavier now, the air was swirling and spinning, and she saw dots before her eyes.

“They don’t leave unless someone listens,” she said. “You know that.”

“Yes,” the figure said softly. “And every time you listen, you forget something of your own.”

Claire froze. She touched her wrist, the place where she used to wear a watch. She could not remember when she had stopped wearing it; she wanted to feel her pulse to know she was alive.

“How many are there?” she asked.

The figure hesitated. “Enough to matter and more than you can help.”

Claire closed her eyes.

That was the rule, then - Don't give all of yourself, there are more than you can help.

She turned back to the basin, lifting her head despite the heaviness and tremor in her hands.

"One more," she said. "Just one more."

The figure did not stop her.

The soul that stepped forward this time was heavier than the others. Older, anchored by something stubborn.

"I hurt too many and stayed too long," it said. "Waiting for forgiveness."

Claire nodded. She knew that weight intimately.

She reached out more slowly now, carefully.

This time, when the memory surged, she felt it tear something loose inside her. A childhood afternoon. The smell of rain on hot pavement. Someone laughing, someone important.

The soul released its final breath. Light rose towards the sky. And something inside Claire went dark.

She collapsed.

The basin dimmed, the remaining souls retreating, murmuring in disappointment and gratitude all at once.

A figure rushed forward, catching her before her head struck stone.

"You cannot keep doing this," it said urgently.

Claire's eyes fluttered open. "I will," she murmured. "Because someone has to."

Her gaze drifted upward, unfocused.

“Just… need to… remember who I am next time.”

The basin went still and somewhere far above. The light dimmed into darkness…

Ray carried Claire in his arms as they continued their journey.

Chapter 30- The Cottage in the Forest

The travelers entered the forest that thinned abruptly. The trees that had pressed close for miles stepped back, their roots loosening their grip on the earth. Light filtered through in softened bands, and the air cleared cleaner, steadier, carrying a scent that made something in Aaron's chest loosen before he understood why.

At the center of the clearing stood a cottage. It was built of stone and dark wood, low and wide, as if it had settled into the land rather than been raised upon it. Smoke curled lazily from its chimney, pale against the trees, and the faintest glow pulsed behind its small, uneven windows. Honey, cinnamon and something baked unmistakably aromatic.

Ray adjusted his grip as Claire's weight sagged further against him. He didn't comment; he simply carried her forward, boots crunching softly over pine needles and leaf mold.

Jonas slowed at the edge of the clearing. "Ah," he said quietly. "Good, we're not too late." The door opened before they knocked. Morwyn stood in the doorway as if she had been waiting for them all morning.

The cottage settled around them like a warm embrace, comforting; it felt like they could finally exhale and let go.

Claire slept for a long time. At first, her rest was shallow, her brow creased, breath uneven, delirious, but Morwyn never hurried it. She moved with quiet purpose, laying cool cloths across Claire's forehead, murmuring words and soft spells. The fire crackled low and steady, its light rising and falling like a living thing.

Jonas sat near the hearth, plucking violin strings, the first note slipped into the room like a sigh, low, unhurried, warm. It wasn't a tune meant to be followed; it wandered instead, circling familiar ground, pausing where the fire popped or where the wind brushed softly against the windows.

The music felt remembered, reminders of times gone by, like something once hummed at the edge of sleep, a lullaby of sorts.

Sage watched from the table, sketching absent shapes in disregarded candles' wax with the end of a charcoal stick. The lines didn't mean anything yet. That was all right. As the music wound through the room, their hand slowed, then stilled, charcoal resting lightly between their fingers.

Ray remained near the hearth, close enough to Claire that he could reach her if she stirred. He sat on the floor with his back against the stone, shield resting at his side, eyes never fully closing. Even at rest, he was listening; the tension in his shoulders had eased, just a fraction, as the melody settled.

The dragon shifted closer to the fire, curling its tail around itself. Its eyes drifted shut, It's heartbeat steady and contained.

Aaron hovered. He didn't know where to put himself now that the danger had passed. He stood, then sat, then stood again, finally perching on the edge of a chair like he might be asked to leave at any moment.

Morwyn noticed, she set a small plate in front of him, honey cakes still warm, steam curling faintly from their surface.

"Eat," she said.

Aaron blinked. “I’m not really hungry.”

“You are,” Morwyn replied. “Trust me.”

He took a bite.

Something loosened in his chest.

They sat in companionable silence for a while, broken only by the soft pop of the fire, the low hum of Jonas’s violin, and the dragon’s occasional huff as it shifted closer to Aaron’s feet.

Finally, Aaron spoke. “I don’t feel different.”

Morwyn didn’t look up from pouring tea. “Good.”

He frowned. “Everyone keeps saying things like that.”

She slid a mug toward him and sat across the table, folding her hands.

“People expect change to be loud,” she said. “Trumpets, fireworks, and a sudden understanding of everything.”

Aaron stared into his tea. “I'm scared I'll do it wrong.”

Morwyn's voice softened. “You will, and then you'll learn,” she continued. “And then you'll try again. That's the whole business of becoming anything worth being.”

“You don’t lead because you know the way,” she said. “You lead because you notice when someone’s fallen behind, and you help others along the way.”

Aaron swallowed, nodding once.

From his spot by the fire, Ray shifted. His shoulders were hunched forward, elbows on his knees, hands clasped tight. He stared at the flames for a long moment before speaking.

“Why us, though?” His voice came out rougher than he meant to. “I mean... really. Why us?”

The question hung in the air.

Sage looked up from where they'd been tracing idle patterns on the table with one finger. “We're just... we're nobody special.” Their voice cracked slightly. “I draw things. Ray picks up trash. Claire…” They gestured helplessly. “We're not heroes.”

Claire shifted slightly onto her side, hair falling forward to hide her face.

Aaron's eyes were suddenly wet. He ducked his head, shoulders curling inward like he was trying to make himself smaller.

The dragon pressed closer to his leg, a low rumble in its chest.

Jonas had stopped playing. The silence felt heavier without the music.

Ray rubbed his face with both hands. “I just... I keep thinking about that distorted weave. About Aaron, almost…” His voice broke; he couldn't finish.

“We're so tired,” Claire whispered. She finally looked up, and her eyes were red-rimmed. “And there's still so much ahead, and I don't know if we're strong enough for this.”

Morwyn let the silence settle for a moment. She didn't rush to fill it with reassurance. She simply sat, hands folded, watching them with eyes that had seen this kind of breaking before, when the weight becomes real, when the fear finally finds its voice.

Then she stood and moved to the kettle, pouring more tea with steady hands. “You're right,” she said quietly. “You are tired, you are scared, and you are, by most measures, quite ordinary.”

She set fresh mugs in front of each of them. “But the Weave doesn't choose heroes,” she continued, settling back into her chair. “It chooses people who notice, who care, and who show up even when they're terrified." Her gaze moved from face to face. "It chose a man who stops his truck to move a turtle off the road, an artist who draws doors because something about them matters, a nurse who sits with the dying long after her shift has ended because someone should remember their names. A musician who plays for coins but gives comfort for free, and a boy who dreams and shows courage and now protects a dragon he just met because it's the right thing to do."

She leaned forward slightly. "The Weave didn't choose you because you're fearless," she said. "It chose you because you are kind and, kindness my dears, is the strongest thread of all."

Ray's jaw worked. He nodded once, roughly, and wiped his eyes. "I'm not crying … your crying," he said under his breath trying to break the tension

Sage took a shaky breath and picked up their mug.

Aaron straightened slightly, the dragon's warmth solid against his leg.

Across the room, Claire stirred. She sat up, appearing unfocused at first. Morwyn was at her side in an instant, pressing a warm cup into her hands.

"Drink," Morwyn said. "Small sips."

Claire obeyed, exhaustion still heavy in her limbs but no longer crushing. The ache inside her, the one she'd carried for years without naming, had eased, gentler now. Like something finally set down.

"I'm sorry," Claire murmured, looking at Ray, "For what?" Ray asked quietly.

"For… needing help."

Morwyn snorted softly. "You're terrible at receiving," she said. "We'll work on it."

Claire managed to make a tired smile.

Sage looked up from the table. “The Weave feels steadier here.”

Morwyn nodded. “For now.”

Jonas placed the violin in its case. “Rest while it holds,” he said.

No one argued. They ate, drank, and, finally slept renewed. Outside, the forest shifted, waiting...

Inside the cottage, five travelers gathered themselves piece by piece, wrapped in firelight, music, nourishment, and shared quiet.

Chapter 31- The Gifts

Morning came quietly.

Light filtered through the cottage windows in pale, honeyed bands, touching the stone floor and warming the air just enough to stir sleep into waking. The fire had burned down to embers, glowing softly, and the forest outside breathed with the slow patience of something awakening.

Claire woke first. She felt… lighter, the sensations in her hands had returned, she felt steadier, as if something inside her had been set back into alignment. Her body still ached, but the ache no longer felt like punishment. It felt like efforts spent.

Morwyn was already moving about the kitchen, as if she had never slept at all. "You're up," she said without turning. "Good. Sit. You'll want to eat before you think too much."

Claire smiled faintly and obeyed. One by one, the others stirred. Ray stretched with a low groan, joints protesting, then checked instinctively that everyone was still there. Sage blinked awake at the table, charcoal smudged across their fingers and cheek, lines of half-remembered drawings etched into the wood beneath their elbow. Aaron woke tangled in a blanket on the floor, the dragon curled protectively against his side, blinking sleepily as the light touched its scales.

Jonas was already outside, violin in hand, playing to the trees. The tune drifted in through the open window, lighter than the night's music, threaded with motion, like a road unfolding.

Morwyn set out three small bundles on the table. Wrapped in cloth, plain and unassuming. "Before you go," she said, finally facing them, "you'll take these."

Aaron frowned. "Are they… magic?" Morwyn snorted. "Everything's magic if you know how to listen. These just happen to listen back."

She gestured to Claire first. Morwyn placed a smooth stone pendant into Claire's palm, cool and heavy, etched faintly in the shape of two hands entwined. "This belonged to a healer long before you," Morwyn said. "It won't stop you from feeling what others carry, but it will remind you of what is yours and what is not." Claire closed her fingers around it, breath catching. "Thank you," she said. "You don't have to carry everything alone," Morwyn added gently.

Next, Morwyn turned to Ray. In his little bundle was a strip of leather, worn soft with age, fastened with a simple iron clasp. "A binding," she said. "Not for strength, but for steadiness. When you raise your shield, it will help you remember why you stand, not just how." Ray nodded once, throat tight. "Thank you." Morwyn met his gaze. "You've always stood between harm and the helpless. Now the land knows it too."

For Sage, Morwyn unfolded a small pouch. Inside lay a single piece of graphite, not charcoal and not quite stone, dark and faintly iridescent. "It won't draw what you see," Morwyn said. "It draws what the Weave is trying to show you. "Sage turned it between their fingers in unmistakable. Awe "So, I won't always understand it?" they asked. Morwyn smiled. "If you did, it wouldn't be worth drawing."

Morwyn sat down in front of Aaron. From beneath the table, she drew out a small, narrow blade wrapped in a dark cloth. When she unfolded it, the metal caught the morning light with a deep, quiet sheen. The dagger was short. Balanced for smaller hands. Its Damascus blade of forged dark steel, faintly veined faintly with silver, as if something older than iron had been folded into it. The handle was the most striking part, curved and pale, unmistakably shaped from a griffin's claw, smooth and grooved where fingers had worn it over time.

Aaron's breath caught. "I…" he hesitated. "I already have the dragon glass." Morwyn nodded. "That was for remembering your courage." She placed the dagger carefully into his hands. "This is for choosing, you decide when or when not to use it." Aaron swallowed, fingers tightening instinctively around the grip. "It's not a weapon meant for battle," Morwyn said firmly. "It won't make you stronger. It won't protect you from every danger." She tapped the blade once with her finger. "But it will remind you that even kings must sometimes stand close to fear and decide what must be cut away, and what must be spared."

Aaron looked down at it, then back up at her. "What if I'm wrong?" Morwyn smiled knowingly. "Then you learn," she said. "And you live with the choice. That's what makes it yours." The dragon leaned in, sniffed the dagger, then huffed softly, not pleased but accepting. Aaron slid the dagger carefully into his belt, movements deliberate, almost ceremonial. He looked very young and, for the first time, very aware.

Morwyn rested two fingers briefly against his forehead. "You won't walk this path perfectly," she said. "But you won't walk it alone." Aaron smiled despite himself.

Last, Morwyn turned toward the doorway. Jonas had stepped inside without sound.

For him, Morwyn offered nothing wrapped. Instead, she said, "I've cleared the path ahead, just a little. Don't waste it." Jonas inclined his head. "I wouldn't dare." She hesitated, then added, "And try not to be late again." Jonas smiled. "No promises."

They gathered near the door, packs shouldered, breath visible in the cool morning air. Morwyn's tone shifted then, subtle, but unmistakable. "The Shadow Maw will stop circling now," she said. "You've moved from curiosity into consequence."

No one spoke. “It feeds on pain, fear, and what has been forgotten,” Morwyn continued. “Names, bonds, and broken promises. It will try to pull you apart, not with force, but by causing doubt. Her eyes rested on Aaron last. “Remember,” she said, “The voices that speak fear and doubt – they are not the truth of you. Remember your strength.” Aaron nodded, gripping the dagger tightly.

Morwyn stepped out of the doorway. The forest beyond waited, changed, watchful, threaded with paths that had not been there before. “Go,” she said. “And don’t rush, the Weave breaks when pressed too hard.”

They stepped out into the morning light. Behind them, the cottage settled once more, smoke thinning into the trees.

Morwyn watched until they were gone. Then she turned back to the quiet hearth and murmured to herself, “May you remember each other… when the world tries to make you forget and tear you apart.”

Chapter 32- The Journey Continues

They left the cottage just after sunrise.

The forest beyond Morwyn's clearing felt different from the way it had the night before. It felt more alert. Dew clung to leaves and low ferns, catching the light in brief flashes that vanished as soon as they were noticed.

The path ahead was narrow. Not overgrown or hidden, just simply tight, as if the land had decided how many could pass at once.

Ray went first, shield on his arm but lowered, boots testing the ground with care. Sage followed, eyes tracking the way the trees leaned subtly inward. Claire walked beside Aaron, slower now, steadier, though the weight of the Basin still lingered behind her eyes.

Jonas brought up the rear, violin case resting against his hip.

The dragon padded at Aaron's heel, tail flicking occasionally, nostrils flaring as it tasted the air.

"This road didn't exist yesterday," Sage said quietly.

Jonas nodded. "The Weave is adjusting."

“To us?” Aaron asked.

“To necessity,” Jonas replied. “Which, is worse.”

They walked in silence for a time. The forest thinned gradually, giving way to rolling ground cut through with long seams of stone and dead trees. The air cooled, carrying the faint scent of muddy water in the distance, deep, and unmoving.

Aaron touched the hilt of the dagger at his belt without meaning to. Morwyn’s words echoed in his mind. “Choosing when not to use it.”

Up ahead, the path forked. Not cleanly, there were no signposts, no clear division, just a subtle pull in two directions. To the left, the ground sloped downward, mist curling low. To the right, the land rose sharply toward broken hills where stone teeth jutted skyward.

Jonas stopped.

“Which way?” Ray asked.

Jonas didn't answer.

Sage crouched, pressing graphite to the ground. The line they drew trembled with uncertainty and strain. “The Weave’s thinner to the left,” they said. “But not broken.”

Claire closed her eyes briefly. “There’s pain both ways,” she said. “But the left… It’s quieter. Like something waiting to expand.”

The dragon growled softly, claws scraping stone, then turned its head toward the rising hills.

Aaron felt it before he understood it, a tug, gentle but insistent, not fear exactly, but responsibility. He hesitated.

Everyone waited. He hated that they were waiting for him to decide. He didn’t want to lead; he just wanted to follow. “I think…” His voice wobbled, then steadied. “I think the left way needs us sooner.”

Ray glanced at Jonas.

Jonas smiled faintly. “Then that’s our road.”

They turned as one. Behind them, the unused path did not fade; it twisted like an old, weather-worn rope. Somewhere far away or perhaps very near, the Shadow Maw shifted, tasting the choice they had made.

The dragon lifted its head, alert.

“Stay close,” said Jonas quietly.

And they walked on, five travelers, one road, the Weave tightening around them with every step.

Chapter 33 – What Should be Severed

There was a distinct pressure shift as if a storm was brewing, the stone beneath their boots was no longer granite or basalt, but something softer. Pale limestone, crumbling at the edges, slick with moisture that had nowhere to go. The air thickened as they continued to walk, heavy and damp, clinging to skin and lungs alike.

The cliffs curved inward, their edges streaked with green and rust-brown stains where water had seeped and pooled for too long. Moss grew in thick, uneven patches, some of it shimmering in the dim light, glowing faintly with luminescence like something half-alive and still breathing. The sea was there, but it did not move, its surface thick with Red tide. Below them, the inlet slowly revealed itself.

The dragon halted, head snapping upward, wings twitching as a low, uneasy sound rumbled from its chest. The pale afternoon glow that had held the inlet steady began to waver, as if something massive was moving between them and the sky.

“Something's coming,” Ray said quietly.

Jonas swore softly. “Oh, crap,” he said. “That’s not good.”

A shadow swept across the inlet, it was vast and deliberate. It passed over them once, twice, circling. The light fractured strangely where it moved, bending wrong, casting shadows that didn't match anything solid.

Then the shadow slowed. It began to merge above the distorted seam, gathering density, taking shape. Its wings were too stiff and shredded, stretched as if pulled by invisible strings. Its scales were dulled and cracked, veins of dark corrosion running through them like rot beneath bark. Threads of thin, shimmering strands of blackened Weave wrapped around its limbs and throat like chains, jerking it through the air in sharp, unnatural movements.

It did not roar. It screamed, a blood-curdling scream. The sound cut through Aaron's chest like glass.

The distorted dragon spiraled lower, wings buckling, crashing into the cliffside above the inlet. Stones exploded outward, sending dust and debris raining down.

"That's a guardian," Sage whispered. "Or it was, I think."

It hung there, half-materialized, as if the world itself was still deciding whether to let it fully exist.

Aaron's breath caught. He couldn't look away. "It's trapped," he said, voice tight. "Those things… those threads, they're hurting it."

Ray shifted his stance, instinctively raising his shield "Kid …"

"I can help," Aaron insisted.

Ray muttered under his breath, "Every terrible idea starts with those three words."

Aaron's dragon growled deep, furious wings unfurling.

"It's trapped," Aaron said again. "Those threads…"

“They’re binding it,” Jonas said. “But not controlling it anymore, not fully.”

Aaron’s heart pounded. “What must be cut.” Running through his mind.

The dagger felt heavy at his side.

He didn’t ask. He ran.

Ray shouted his name, but Aaron was already climbing the rocks at the edge of the inlet, scrambling upward with reckless determination. The dragon followed, growing, unfolding his wings, becoming his magnificent size………. swooping under Aaron, lifting him with a rush of heat and wind just as the distorted guardian lunged again.

Aaron clung to the dragon’s neck, eyes stinging, fear roaring in his ears. “Get me closer!” he yelled.

The dragon hesitated, then surged upward. They rose into the sky, wind tearing at Aaron’s clothes, the distorted dragon wheeling toward them, eyes wild, unfocused, burning with pain.

The black threads shimmered, taut as wire. Aaron didn’t think. He cut. The dagger flashed once, clean and decisive slicing through the binding strands.

The threads snapped. For a single heartbeat, the distorted dragon went still. Then it screamed again louder, angrier. The rot surged. The distortion wasn’t released it was revealed. The dragon’s body twisted and contorted violently, shadow spilling outward, wings snapping wide as the creature let out a scream filled with pain. Aaron’s stomach lurched.

Jonas’s voice carried up from below, sharp with urgency. “Aaron, that wasn’t binding it, that was containing it!”

Aaron could not hear him; the bronze dragon moved without hesitation. The distorted dragon lunged again.

The sky exploded into motion. Fire and shadow collided, the clash echoing across the inlet as the two dragons tore through the air, one blazing and alive, the other shrieking, unraveling, held together only by rage and rot.

Aaron clung tight, terror and awe crashing together in his chest. Flames seared the sky. Shadows recoiled.

Then the distorted dragon struck again, jaws snapping, but its movements were erratic, desperate. The Weave threads are gone now, leaving it unbalanced, incomplete.

Aaron's dragon roared. It drove forward, fire pouring from its throat, wild and focused, piercing straight through the distortion at the creature's core.

The twisted dragon convulsed once, twice, then shattered into ash and dark light, scattering on the wind like burnt paper.

Silence followed, and the sky cleared.

The dragon landed, and Aaron slid down, legs shaking so badly he couldn't stand. He couldn't breathe. His chest felt too tight, like something was squeezing all the air out, and his hands were shaking. His whole body was trembling. He tried to say something; he tried to apologize, but the words stuck in his throat like stones.

"I…" His voice cracked. "I'm sorry, I…I thought…"

He couldn't finish. His eyes burned, and he blinked hard, staring at Ray's shirt because he couldn't look up. Couldn't look at any of them. What if they were mad? What if Jonas was disappointed? What if Ray and the others had gotten hurt because Aaron was stupid and didn't listen, and just…,he knew he just did something without thinking?

"I thought I was helping," he whispered, and his voice sounded so small.

His throat was dry and hoarse. He wanted to disappear. He wanted to take it all back. They could have been hurt or worse, and it would have been Aaron's fault.

Jonas knelt in front of him.

Aaron kept his eyes down, fixed on the ground. His vision blurred. “You acted,” Jonas said, voice calm and steady. “And you learned, and this time you made the right decision, but next time you act impulsively might not be the right choice.”

Aaron's breath hitched. He risked a glance up just for a second, and Jonas's expression wasn't angry, it wasn't disappointment, it was just... steady. Like he meant it.

But Aaron's chest still felt tight. Because he hadn't made the right decision at first. He'd messed up. He'd almost made everything worse.

Claire stepped closer, placing a hand over Aaron's chest, grounding him. The warmth helped a little. Sage stared at the sky, graphite clenched tight. “Most people don't act,” Sage said quietly, “most people wait for someone else to act first.”

Aaron looked at the dagger in his hand. His fingers were still shaking. He slid it back into his belt with care, trying to be gentle even though his hands wouldn't stop trembling.

Morwyn’s words echoed in his mind. The dragon nudged him gently, a low, reassuring huff. Aaron leaned into it, just for a moment, and felt his breathing slow down.

Jonas added,“The land will remember what you just did -what you're made of. So will the Shadow Maw.”

Aaron swallowed hard. His throat still hurt, but he managed to nod.

“I'll think a little more carefully next time before I act,” he said quietly. He meant it. He really, really meant it.

Jonas nodded. “Good.”

The inlet below shimmered faintly as the distortion receded, no longer spreading.

The first cut had been made, and a cost had been paid.

Chapter 34 – What Lingers

They walked for a long time after the sky cleared. No one rushed to speak. The land itself seemed quieter now, as if it were listening to what would be said next.

The path twisted downward again, through hills and valleys, over rocks and stones.

Aaron kept his eyes on the ground.

Finally, Jonas spoke. "What you saw up there," he said, voice carrying easily in the open air, "wasn't distortion beginning."

Aaron flinched. "It was a distortion failing," Jonas continued. "And sometimes that is worse."

Sage looked up sharply. "Failing?"

Jonas nodded. "Distortion isn't a thing on its own. It's a condition of corruption. It happens when the Weave is strained long enough that it forgets how to let go."

Ray frowned. "Let go of what?"

"Pain," Claire said quietly.

Jonas gave her a nod of acknowledgment. "Exactly."

He walked a few steps ahead, tapping his bow lightly against the violin strings. The note wavered, uneven.

“When grief, fear, regret, and shame are held too tightly for too long, they don’t fade,” Jonas said. “They sink. They warp the threads around themselves, they suffocate hope and joy.”

Sage’s graphite traced a line in the air unconsciously. “Like stress fractures.”

“Like scars that never heal,” Jonas added. “The guardian you saw was meant to protect this place. But it stayed long after it should have rested.”

Aaron swallowed. “So… cutting the threads…”

“Would have freed it,” Jonas said gently, “if there had been anything left to free.”

The dragon huffed softly, smoke curling from its nostrils.

“The tragedy,” Jonas went on, “is that distortion often looks like something that can be saved.”

No one questioned him. They kept walking on.

The Inn appeared where the path bent inward, tucked unnaturally close to the rock face. By all appearances, it should not have been there.

That was the first thing Sage noticed, not wrongness, but the improbability. The land around it bore no signs of use, no worn stones, no trampled, grass and no scented trail.

Yet the building itself looked inviting enough. Warm light glowed through its windows. Smoke rose from the chimney in a steady line. A wooden sign creaked gently in the breeze, its lettering faded but readable: THE WAYFARER’S REST INN

Aaron’s stomach tightened. “That looks… almost normal."

Jonas stopped. “That’s the problem,” he said.

They approached cautiously. As they drew closer, sound reached them of low conversation, a drone of voices all talking over each other, and the clink of mugs. A fiddle played somewhere inside, repeating a tune that looped and skipped off key and out of tune. The fiddler added a flourish where there shouldn’t have been one. A stumble of rhythm. A playful exaggeration of the tune’s sweetest turn.

Claire’s breath caught. She knew that sound. Not the tune but the feeling of it. It stalled as if the sound was holding, waiting.

Ray reached the door first and pushed it open.

Warmth spilled out, along with the smell of bread and stew. Inside, the inn was full. Men and women sat at tables mid-conversation. A barmaid leaned forward with a pitcher, frozen halfway through pouring. A man laughed, mouth open, eyes bright.

Then the moment passed. The pitcher tipped. Ale spilled into the mug. Laughter resumed.

No one noticed the travelers.

Sage whispered, “Does anyone else see their eyes?”

“Yes, they look dead,” Ray said quietly.

They stepped fully inside, and the tune restarted.

Jonas had gone very still.

“The tune,” he said quietly.

Sage turned toward him. “What about it?”

Jonas tilted his head, listening as the fiddle began the exact same opening phrase, the same tempo, the same hesitation before the third note again. The sounds around them did not match the movements; everything was out of time.

"I've heard this before," Jonas said. "Not here, long ago."

The fiddle skipped and reset. "The loop isn't anchored to the people," Jonas continued. "It's anchored to the moment, a memory that never finished."

Ray's jaw tightened. "So how do we end it?" He lifted his shield, ready to ram.

Jonas smiled faintly. "Easy, big fella, you don't break a loop with force."

The barmaid passed them again, pitcher raised, eyes unfocused.

"You interrupt it," Jonas said. "With something that doesn't belong."

Aaron looked around. "Like… what?"

Jonas's smile widened just a little. "Laughter and joy."

Sage blinked. "You're kidding."

"I never kid about music," Jonas replied.

Before anyone could stop him, Jonas stepped into the center of the room, lifted his violin, and began to play. He mirrored the opening phrase, close enough to be mistaken for harmony. Then something went intentionally wrong. The cheer in the melody thinned. Smiles stalled. A laugh died halfway out of someone's mouth.

Jonas lingered, letting the sound stretch until it felt uncomfortable, like a joke told too often. A man at the bar shifted. The barmaid overpoured, ale sloshing onto the counter. Jonas paused mid-phrase and held the silence just long enough to be uncomfortable, then resumed with a note so sharp and bright it made Aaron wince. When he played again, the note hit like a pinprick in the inner ears. Aaron flinched. "There," Jonas said. "That's the note you didn't want anyone to notice. "Sage clapped a hand over their mouth, shoulders shaking, suppressing a laugh.

A woman near the bar blinked; the unseen fiddler tried to recover, speeding up to catch the loop. Jonas matched him then kept going, racing ahead with exaggerated enthusiasm until the melody sounded frantic, stumbling over itself. "Oh dear," Jonas said sarcastically. "Was that too fast? My apologies." He slowed again. Comically. Each note is drawn out with theatrical precision. A man at a corner table frowned, his mug halfway to his lips and the barmaid missed the pour completely, the ale sloshing onto the counter.

"There we are," Jonas said. "Much better. Really captures the... what would you call it? The self-satisfaction."

Claire pressed both hands over their mouth, muffling a giggle.

The fiddler missed a note entirely.

Aaron's lips twitched. Claire and Sage began to giggle openly at the sight.

Jonas took that as permission. He launched into something that could barely be called a melody, all wrong turns and dramatic pauses, notes that clashed with cheerful violence. He added a trill that belonged to a funeral march, then followed it with a bounce that belonged at a children's party, then a sailor's shanty, a tune for tapping feet, then a melody that refused to behave. It danced where it should have marched, it paused mid-phrase, then resumed with exaggerated enthusiasm.

"I've heard drunk goats keep better time," Ray announced. "And they had more humility about it," Jonas smirked in his direction and played a note so absurdly high it squeaked.

The dragon who had been watching with increasing agitation let out a sharp, indignant squawk and flapped both wings, nearly knocking Aaron sideways. Jonas raised an eyebrow at him and leaned into the ridiculousness.

A woman near the hearth let out a startled, drunk snort, disbelieving, almost a bark, then froze, hand flying to her mouth as if she'd committed a crime, but the damage was done. Aaron laughed louder now, a grunt escaping his mouth.

Jonas played one final note long, wavering, and utterly pitiful. Then he stopped. Lowered his violin and smiled. That did it. The room wobbled. The fiddle screeched and cut off entirely. Silence crashed down.

Then someone laughed again, longer this time. The sound rippled hesitantly, uncertain, then spread, fragile but real. The loop collapsed, and silence fell hard.

For the first time since they'd entered, the patrons moved freely, slowly, shakily, as if waking from a dream.

Claire's breath came with urgency. "Now," she said. "Before it starts again."

Sage was already moving. They had noticed it earlier a seam in the back wall where the shadows didn't quite behave. While everyone else was distracted by laughter, Sage pressed their palm against the wood.

It shifted. The narrow door swung inward, hidden behind stacked crates. Cold, stale air spilled out. The smell hit them immediately of damp stone, rot, and something sharp and stagnant beneath it.

Ray stepped forward onto the staircase and raised his shield. "I'll go first."

They descended into darkness. The basement was out of place, quieter than the inn above. Stone walls are slick with moisture. Threads of dark Weave crawled across the ceiling like veins, pulsing faintly.

At the center of the room, a creature crouched. Small and twisted. Not quite human, not quite animal. It's back hunched with a protruding spine, limbs drawn tight to its almost colorless, very pale, bluish skin, it cowered backwards into the corner as if trying to disappear into itself. Blackened threads pierced its form, running into the walls like roots.

It whimpered when they entered. Claire's heart broke open. The pull was immediate, a tide of loneliness and despair so vast it threatened to drown her where she stood. Her chest tightened. Her breath shortened. Every instinct she'd learned to trust screamed at her to step back, to shield herself, to remember what Morwyn had taught her about boundaries.

“It's been feeding on this,” she whispered. Pointing to a mangled mess on the floor.

Jonas nodded grimly. " Sustaining itself on despair."

Aaron stepped forward without thinking.

Ray caught his shoulder gently. “Easy.”

The creature lifted its head.

“It didn't cause the loop," Sage said softly. “It's what was left behind when the loop broke.”

Claire took a step forward, then stopped. She could feel it already; touching it would cost something. The weight of centuries pressing against her ribs. The hollow ache that would settle into her bones and stay there. She'd spent so long learning not to disappear into other people's pain. This would be worse.

“Claire.” Ray's voice was quiet. Careful. “You don't have to…”

“I know,” she said. But she knelt anyway, slowly, ignoring the cold stone biting into her knees. Her hands trembled as she lowered them toward the creature's chest.

“It remembers pain,” she said. “But not who caused it or why.”

Claire hesitated and moved slowly, her fingers hovering just above the matted fur and corrupted flesh. She could already feel the edges of it, the vast, terrible emptiness waiting to pour into her.

She thought of the stone pendant resting against her chest. You don't have to take everything with you. But sometimes you did. Sometimes the only way was through.

Claire reached out carefully, deliberately, and placed her hand just above its chest. "It's all right," she said. "You don't have to hold onto this anymore."

The threads tightened, then trembled above them, the inn creaked, time shifting, unsticking.

Jonas raised his bow, drawing a single, steady note.

The creature exhaled and disintegrated into a pile of light grey ash. And the basement grew very, very still.

When they returned upstairs, the inn was transformed. The repeating motions stopped. The figures still echo. Their eyes, still hollow, turned toward them in serene stillness. They bowed. The innkeeper spoke, "Thank you, travelers." His form shimmered, becoming translucent. "Our time here is done …we can rest now."

One by one, the echoes dissolved into soft light, drifting upward like fireflies toward the rafters.

Claire wiped her cheek. "They were trapped for so long…"

Sage placed a hand on her shoulder. "Not anymore."

Jonas closed his violin case with a click. "Another fracture mended."

Ray cracked his knuckles. "Where to next?"

Aaron stepped forward and said confidently. "Wherever the next shard leads."

The dragon chirped approvingly, wings fluttering.

And as they left the inn, the now-peaceful lanterns flickered behind them like blessings. The forest ahead waited, twisted, dangerous, alive

But they were ready.

Chapter 35 – When the Road Answers Back

Mist clung low to the ground, curling around the roots of the trees like something reluctant to let go. Beyond the band of trees, the land lay flat and spread out into a wide-open wasteland of stones and broken, scorched trees that looked like they had been ravaged by fire. Farther still, cliffs rose in layered plates, their faces streaked with dark seams where the Weave had thinned.

The lake Jonas had spoken of lay beyond those cliffs. Beautiful once, serene. Wounded now.

Sage stood at the edge of the outcrop; they stared off into the void of swirling black and violet. Threads snapped around their vision like dying stars.

A figure appeared faceless, robed in unraveling strands. Sage gasped. Vaeron the Unraveller. Its voice echoed like torn cloth. "You cannot mend what you do not understand."

Sage caught her breath: "The Weave fractures because the realm is dying. Because people have forgotten kindness, they live and feed off greed and fear. And soon, the five threads will break as well." The voice continued.

Then the scene shifted. Sage gasped and stepped back, unsteady. "This path isn't broken," they said finally. "It's… been torn apart by a destructive being."

Sage then crouched and touched the earth. A thin charcoal line bled outward from their fingers, sketching itself across stone and soil. It curved and doubled back, then vanished entirely. "We're being turned around," Sage said. "Not blocked but purposely misled."

Ray frowned. "By what?"

Jonas tilted his head. "By something that doesn't want us reaching the water."

The words settled uneasily among them. The lake!

Aaron shifted his weight. "That's where the tear is, isn't it?"

Jonas nodded. "One of them."

The dragon stirred, wings twitching. A faint growl rolled from its chest in recognition.

Claire closed her eyes. She could feel it, the land's discomfort and confusion, the low murmur of strain beneath stone and root. Jonas lifted his violin and drew the bow lightly across the strings. Just one note. The sound did not echo. It visibly moved the air.

Ahead, the mist thinned, rearranging itself into a narrow passage between trees that revealed more stone outcroppings that hadn't been there moments before.

Ray exhaled slowly. "Well. That's new."

Jonas smiled faintly. "The road has decided to answer back."

Aaron tightened his grip on the dagger at his side. "Does that mean we're close?"

Jonas lowered the violin. “It means,” he said, “that the land has noticed we’re serious.”

They set off together. Behind them, the forest, outcrop, and Inn faded into the distance. Ahead, the path curved towards muddy shores and treacherous water. And somewhere beyond that, the Weave waited, frayed, exposed, and running out of time.

Chapter 36- The Broken Compass

As they pushed deeper into the thinning fog, Ray's boot struck something half-buried beneath the loose gravel.

He stopped and crouched. Rust-flaked and warped, a circular object protruded from the gravel. "Well," he muttered, digging it out and brushing the dirt away, "what have we here? That's either treasure or tetanus."

He turned it over in his palm. The glass was cracked, spider-webbed from a single impact. The needle lay bent to one side, useless, or so it seemed. Strange runes ringed the casing, etched deep, older than the forest itself.

Sage crouched beside him, eyes narrowing. "It's not any compass I've ever seen."

Aaron tilted his head. "Does it work?"

"I'd say no," Ray said. "By the looks of it. Unless North has recently given up."

Jonas leaned closer and touched it with his fingers. "It's from the Old Realm. It doesn't find north, it finds truth."

Claire asked quietly, "Why was it here?"

"Lost," Jonas murmured. "Like everything else affected by the Unraveling, or we have an unknown ally."

Ray held the compass. It felt flesh warm. "I've always had a knack for finding lost things," he said, as if stating a fac, he'd only just realized.

No one argued. They moved on. Ray flipped the compass absently as they walked. The crack in the glass glimmered. Then it began to glow. The needle twitched. Once, twice, it began to spin, slow at first, like it was remembering itself, then faster and faster until it snapped to attention, pointing straight into a wall of fog thick with gloom.

Aaron's eyes widened. "It works!"

Ray grimaced. "Why is it always me who finds the weird stuff?"

Jonas smiled, small but knowing. "Because protectors carry direction inside them. Even when they think they've lost it, and because you picked it up."

Ray shrugged. Then he squared his shoulders. "Alright then," he said. "Guess I'll lead."

They followed the compass deeper into the forest as it glowed in Ray's hand.

Aaron's dragon growled low.

Sage's graphite shard pulsed in warning.

Then the mist became thick like mud, and the forest grew very quiet. Shapes emerged. Their hearts stopped. At first, they thought they were Shadows Mews. Then the shadows stepped forward, and the world shifted. The ground angled strangely beneath their feet. Gravity felt undecided. The air pressed in from all sides, as if time itself were watching. Five figures appeared. They looked like people; they looked like the five of them, but very distorted.

Aaron saw a taller boy, older, hollow-eyed, no dragon by his side. The reflection stared at him with resentment.

"You could have been great," it hissed. "If you weren't so afraid." "I'm not afraid," Aaron snapped, sounding braver than he felt. "Who are you?" There was no answer.

Sage faced a version of themself drained of color, greyscale like an old photograph. Their hands were empty. Their eyes are dull. "No brilliance left," it sneered. "Just failure...."

Ray's reflection was even worse. It was bent and broken. Tears carved permanent lines down his face. His wife's voice echoed from nowhere and everywhere. "You weren't strong enough to save me. You cowered and turned away. You always did." Ray's shield dipped.

Claire gasped as her reflection stepped forward, luminous and cold, surrounded by the phantoms of patients she had lost. "You don't heal," it whispered. "You're not good enough. Impostor."

Jonas's reflection bled sound notes leaking from its chest like open wounds. "Your music ends," it mocked. "The Weave ends. You end."

The reflections advanced. Smiling wickedly.

"Don't engage!" Jonas shouted. "They're just illusions!"

Ray roared, raising his shield. "Stay back or I'll...!" His reflection lunged. Ray closed his eyes. Braced, but nothing hit. He opened them, and all he could see was sand. Endless, fine sand beneath his feet. No forest, no reflections, and no companions. "Aaron?" Ray spun. "Sage, Claire, Jonas?"

But they were elsewhere.

Aaron wrapped himself around the dragon as the reflections rushed him. He waited for impact, but nothing happened. He looked up, all he could see was Ray standing a little away from him, both surrounded by sand. "I was waiting," he whispered. "And… nothing." "Where's my dragon? "He was just in my arms…"

Sage slashed symbols through the air, painted defenses that met no resistance. Claire raised her hands, light flaring… Then silence.

They stood together again, all on a mound of sand, breathing hard. But something was wrong. "We were there…," Ray said slowly. "And now we're here…." Claire's voice shook. "Where is Jonas and the dragon. We must find them." Ray lifted the compass. The needle spun wildly faster and faster, then locked onto a direction.

"That way!" Aaron shouted, sprinting forward

THUCK.

He slammed into something invisible and solid. A glass wall. Dazed, the world rang in his ears. And outside. Jonas stood apart. Silently feeling, listening, the ground trembled. The mist tore open like a wound, the earth splitting beneath it as a trapdoor opened. An eight-legged creature crawled out. Clockwork fused with bone. Gears ticking where flesh should be. A spiral of sand fell upward where its face should be, behind it, hundreds of eyes blinking in and out of existence.

A golden cord lashed outward, wrapping the dragon mid-lunge, binding its wings and jaws. It roared once, muffled, struggling uselessly.

Behind the creature stood a huge hourglass, and inside the glass stood Ray, Claire, Sage, and Aaron, trapped. Moments flickered. Past over present, molded and stretched. Jonas's jaw tightened. "A Time-Devourer." The reflections dissolved into the creature's spiral.

Aaron's voice echoed faintly from inside the glass. "I don't know what's happening… where are we? And my head hurts." He rubbed the bump forming above his right eye.

Sage stepped forward, placing a finger against the glass. They traced the curve, walking until they returned to where they started. “I think we’re trapped in something,” they said quietly. “I’m just not sure what.”

“I don’t like the looks of this,” Ray muttered. “I don’t do trapped very well.”

Outside the hourglass, Jonas faced the creature he could not see. It stalked behind him, whispering. “Your friends are lost; the sands of time will see to them.”

Jonas did not cower. He turned slowly. “I’ve dealt with things like you before, Time-Devourer. You don’t frighten me.”

“Think again, music man.” The creature used its spine-covered hairy leg to flick a switch embedded in its shoulder.

Inside the hourglass… “It’s raining,” Aaron said. “No, wait,” he corrected, panic snapping into his voice. “That’s not rain. That’s sand!”

Above them, the hourglass had awakened. The grains began to fall steadily, murmuring as they struck the growing mound at their feet.

“How do we stop it?” Claire cried.

Ray looked up, then down at the sand already covering his boots. “Okay,” he said tightly, “new rule if anyone ever suggests walking into mysterious fog again, we say no.” The sand reached Aaron’s ankles.

Outside the glass, the creature circled Jonas, unseen but felt. “Your friends are lost,” it hissed. “The sands will finish what time began.”

Jonas raised the violin. The first note cut through the air, it cut out suddenly, vanishing as if it had never been played. The hourglass barely shuddered. Inside, the sand surged faster.

"No!" Sage shouted. "Stop moving! something's making it fall faster!"

Jonas stiffened. The creature circled. He could feel it displacing air as it moved. The air pulsed against his skin in uneven beats. His reflection's words crawled back into his mind. "The music ends."

The creature lunged. Jonas barely ducked and rolled to the side, something tore past his shoulder. The bow slipped from his fingers, clattering across gravel.

Inside the hourglass, sand swallowed Aaron's boots.

Jonas dove forward, feeling his way, snatching the bow back as another invisible limb struck where his head had been. He placed his bow once again, this time listening more intently. The sound vibrations moved from his ears through his skull, running down his arms to his fingertips. The sounds of falling sand. He set the bow to the strings.

The creature shrieked as the first sustained note held, refusing to end. Inside the hourglass, the sand faltered.

The creature slammed into him. Jonas staggered, nearly dropping the violin. The note broke. The sand surged again.

Aaron disappeared to the knees.

Jonas planted his feet. Blood ran warm along his knuckles where the strings had cut him. He drew the bow again. This time, he layered the sound. One tone became two, two bent into a third, and the hourglass began to resonate. The glass sang.

The creature cried a sound like clocks shattering underwater. It lashed out wildly, striking out at Jonas, through space, through beats that were no longer there.

Ray swallowed. "Alright. Punching time didn't work. The magic light didn't work. I'm guessing yelling won't help either." Aaron gave a nervous laugh. "I can try screaming?"

Jonas closed his eyes. "It's not sound," he murmured. "It's broken sound. Discord without intent." He made the sound deeper. The vibration made the sand dance and shift at the bottom of the glass prison, the hum of the glass, and the stuttering pulse of the trapped moments.

Cracks appeared like spider-webs across the glass.

Ray felt the vibration under his boots. "Oh," he breathed. "That's new, wait, that's Jonas."

The hourglass resonated, and the sand lifted, suspended in the air.

Jonas drove the sound deeper; he pulled the final harmonic tight. The glass sang, then it shattered, light and sand exploded outward. The creature recoiled and screamed, its spiral unraveling, its hundreds of eyes blinking out of sequence. Light and sand burst outward from its face. The spider came apart in a storm of gears, bone, and dust that dissolved before touching the ground. The hourglass collapsed into glittering fragments. Time snapped back into place. Silence. Jonas lowered the violin with shaking hands.

The dragon's eyes glowed as the golden cords fell away. They stood together again, coughing, dusted in gold. Aaron rubbed his head. "I really don't like time anymore."

Ray looked at the broken glass, then at Jonas. "So… next time we encounter ancient cosmic artifacts, we try music first."

Jonas allowed himself a weary smile. The landscape breathed again. The compass murmured once again in Ray's hand.

Claire brushed sand from her sleeves. "That was the tricky trial, wasn't it?"

Jonas nodded. "The Weave tests your resolve, to see how you grow from challenges."

The ground shifted and smoothed out. Ahead, stone spiral steps rose from the earth, rearranging into a new path.

Ray sighed. “Please don’t be another container.”

Together, they stepped forward deeper into the Valley of Lost Time.

Chapter 37 – The Broken Arch

The shifting valley finally released them into an open clearing. Here, reality felt… thin.

Stone pillars spiraled upward like ribs of a dead giant. Silver threads hung slack between them, frayed and drifting like an old fishing net. In the center stood the Broken Arch. It was enormous, at least four stories high, carved from Malachite, veined with threads of silver light. But the arch was shattered on one side, split down the other side so deeply it looked ready to collapse at any moment. The space within it was not empty.

It was a void of darkness and shadow. A place where nothing lived. The air around it buzzed with a high, sickening hum.

Aaron pulled the dragon closer. "It feels wrong."

Claire nodded. "Everything here feels wound too tight."

Ray raised his shield, as if it could defend against the absence in before them. Sage took a step closer, graphite shard glowing. Jonas simply looked ahead, his expression grave. "The Weave tore here," he murmured. "Completely." Sage shivered. "Is this where the shards fell?"

” No,” Jonas replied softly. “This is where something else broke, I’m not sure what yet.” The dragon growled low, its scaled wings shivering.

The Broken Arch groaned once, a ripple of pure formlessness. And then the ground beneath them loosened. A staircase appeared, made of stone steps that spiraled upward, glowing faintly, shaped with impossible geometry. They rose higher and higher until lost in distant clouds. None of them had seen it appear. It was simply there now, as though it had always existed.

Claire frowned. “That wasn’t here a moment ago.”

Ray scowled. “I don’t trust floating stairs.”

Aaron tilted his head. “Maybe the Weave is up there?”

Jonas didn’t answer immediately. He reached out and touched the first step.

His finger passed through it was like touching smoke.

“It’s a mirage,” Jonas said quietly.

Claire reached out, and her hand met solid stone.

Jonas blinked, “I think it adapts to each of us differently. Illusion for one, real for another.”

Sage’s eyes widened. “So how do we know what’s actually real and what’s not?”

Ray’s compass vibrated violently. The needle swung upward, pointing at the stairs.

Aaron stepped forward, picking the dragon up into his arms. “I think… we’re supposed to climb.”

Claire took his arm and held him back, “No, not alone.”

They placed their feet on the first step. It held.

Ray followed, shield over his back. Sage next, muttering under their breath. Jonas came last, violin case thumping lightly against his hip.

Halfway up, Aaron paused. "Guys does the air feel weird?"

YES!

The answer came not from words, but from the shift of reality. The sky flickered, and the arch pulsed. Then all of a sudden, the staircase tilted. They were no longer ascending, now they were descending, no, ascending again, then sideways. Gravity bent and re-bent as if the valley were laughing.

Sage screamed, "This isn't a staircase, it's a trap!"

Ray's shield slammed into stone as he tried to anchor himself. Claire grabbed Aaron, pulling him and the dragon closer. Jonas dug his fingers into the railing, which melted into mist.

Aaron shouted, panicked, "We're going the wrong way, we're going to fall!"

The dragon shrieked, wings unfolding, its eyes fixated, and it saw something the others couldn't.

It leapt from Aaron's arms and began to grow mid-air, wings flaring molten copper.

It dove past them, slicing through the warped structures. A blast of fire erupted from its mouth, the air caught fire, the clouds flared like dry silk, dissolving into nothing, revealing the truth: A hidden pathway beneath the distorted stairs, winding downward behind a veil of the mirage.

Jonas gasped. "The path goes down, not up! The arch is inverted!"

Claire shouted, "The mirages want us climbing into the void!"

Ray pushed off the tilting stair. "We have to move! Follow the dragon!"

The staircase flickered out from under them. Stones crumbled into dust.

Sage nearly slipped into nothingness, but Ray caught their wrist. Aaron held onto Claire's hand more tightly, Claire gripping Jonas's sleeve.

They slid, scrambled, and fell in a coordinated chaos toward the dragon's firelit path.

The true stairs, worn and cracked, descending into the heart beneath the arch, revealed themselves fully.

They landed with a thud on the top landing of the staircase.

Jonas said in awe. "The dragon… sees through the deception."

Aaron puffed his chest slightly. "He's pretty amazing."

The dragon chirped proudly.

Once they steadied themselves on the true stairway, the mirages collapsed behind them with a sound like a sigh or a muffled scream. The descent was steep and spiraling. Cold wind rose from below, carrying whispers of something archaic and wounded.

Claire tightened her grip on Aaron. "Be careful."

Sage's graphite flickered, casting spiraling colors across the stone. Ray walked ahead, shield raised, compass glowing steadily. Jonas brought up the rear, steps slow and deliberate.

Aaron's dragon flew ahead, weaving like a torch through the dark.

The stairway ended in a vast underground hall, a space carved out of Jade, Amethyst, Garnet, Malachite, and Hematite with veins of silvered stone. Web-like cracks pulsed faint crimson along the walls.

The dragon landed beside Aaron, staring at a circular platform in the center of the room.

A heartbeat. Slow, steady, enormous could be heard.

The Weave itself pulsed beneath the platform.

Jonas inhaled sharply. "We've reached the heart of the tower."

Claire whispered, "It feels… living."

Ray tightened his shield strap. "And angry."

Sage whispered, "Or afraid."

The dragon stood next to the group and growled softly.

Aaron stepped forward, eyes wide. "What now?"

Jonas answered, voice hushed: "Now we meet whatever guards the heart."

The chamber trembled. A shadow stirred behind the Weave-platform. It was large, broken, and waiting.

The next guardian…

Chapter 38 -The Next Guardian

The chamber pulsed like a beating heart, slow, heavy, and uneven. DA-DOOM…DA-DOOM

Aaron stepped closer to the platform of woven silver threads. His dragon crouched low, hackles raised. The others formed a protective semicircle behind him, Ray's shield glowing faintly, Sage's graphite humming with color, Claire's palms shimmering, Jonas's violin case rattling a warning.

Then the darkness behind the platform moved. Stone cracked. And the air thickened.
something massive pulled itself free from the shadows.

A griffin emerged; it was not like the smaller, distorted guardian from before. This one was colossal. The hind legs, tail, and head of a ferocious lion, it had wings and talons of an eagle, it had huge claws and a beak that could tear you apart, its skin was blackened like burnt metal armor, each plate cracked with leaking red light. The distortion spiraled across its body in jagged patterns, like claws that had raked reality itself.

Its eyes were hollow red circles, and wrapped around its chest was a shattered thread of the Weave, the shard they sought. Embedded deep, pulsating erratically.

Claire gasped. “It’s bound to the shard.”

Jonas murmured, “Guardians protect the Weave at any cost. Even distorted ones… it remembers its duty.”

Ray braced himself. “Then we have to free it.”

The distorted guardian lifted its head; the entire chamber shook with its roar.

Aaron stumbled backward as his dragon stepped forward.

The small dragon’s body glowed, then it began to grow, its wings expanded to twice their size.
Fire curled around its throat in spiraling patterns, and a low growl rippled through the chamber, deeper than its size should allow.

Sage whispered, “It’s… transforming again.”

Jonas nodded sharply. “Because Aaron needs it.”

Aaron touched his dragon’s flank. “Don’t get hurt.”

The dragon nuzzled him once, a promise, then leapt into the air.

Its body stretched mid-flight scales, brightening from bronze to molten gold, horns sweeping backward in elegant curves, its tail lengthening with a whip-crack of glowing heat. It landed on the platform, now fully grown, wings expansive enough to stir wind cyclones through the room.

The distorted guardian roared in recognition. A challenge. Aaron’s dragon roared back a command. The battle began. The distorted guardian lunged, beak opening with a hiss of jagged energy. The young dragon shot upward, flames bursting from its mouth to intercept the strike. Heat collided with shadow-fire, shaking the chamber, and sparks flew in every direction.

Ray lifted his shield to block falling debris.
Claire anchored herself with steady breathing, placing one hand on her chest and the other extended toward the fight, projecting calm energy.
Sage painted a sigil of protection in the air, blue pigment forming a dome around them.
Jonas listened to the rhythm of the two guardians' movements, analyzing their patterns.

Aaron, trembling but determined, whispered: "You can win this."

The dragon heard him. The distorted guardian slammed its massive tail across the floor. A shockwave rippled outward, knocking everyone but Ray off their feet. The bronze dragon dove, dodging a blast of distorted sound waves that tore off part of the ceiling. The Griffin changed direction.

Sage shouted, "Aaron, it's aiming for you!"

Then the guardian lunged, talons splayed, ready to rip and tear. It seized a sharp Jaggard crystal, and sent it with intent, directly at Aaron…

The Weave platform glowed; air vibrated with impending destruction. The heat rose.

And Aaron froze like a deer in the headlights.

But Claire ran ahead of him, raising her hands. "NO!"

Her voice rang with power. Her gift flared into full pure protection mode

The Jaggard crystal struck her shield of light and shattered into millions of shards, crashing harmlessly against the chamber walls.

Claire staggered, but she held.

Ray roared, charging forward and slamming his shield into the Griffin's foreleg. The ruby embedded within pulsed, sending a wave of force through the guardian. It stumbled.

Jonas opened the violin case. "Time to turn the tide." He said.

He began playing a sharp, ascending phrase, a melody that stunned the Griffin causing it to lose focus and be disoriented for just a moment. The Griffin shrieked, clutching its head. The Weave-shard embedded in its chest pulsed violently. Aaron's dragon landed on its back, claws digging into blackened feathers. Flying up into the sky, aiming for the sunlight above the clouds, which caused the griffin to scream in pain as its breast plate tore open, revealing the anchor holding the shard.

The moment the anchor was exposed, the chamber reacted. Cracks split across the walls.
The heartbeat of the realm grew frantic, silver threads snapped overhead, and the floor buckled.

Sage shouted, "Jonas, the melody's destabilizing the chamber!"

Jonas kept playing. "That's the point! It's severing the distortion, keep fighting!"

Ray braced against falling stone.
Claire ran to pull Aaron away from the platform.
Aaron shouted, "The shard, we have to get the shard!"

The guardian, weakened but still colossal, reared back for a final attack.

Aaron's dragon leapt from its back, slamming a burst of white-blue fire directly onto the shard.

The distortion shattered. A shockwave blasted outward. The massive guardian collapsed onto the stone, eyes dimming, distortion evaporating from its scales. Beneath the soot and scars, feathered patterns re-emerged, faint but pure.

The smaller guardian, their dragon, landed beside it, nudging its snout gently against the fallen elder.

Claire placed her hand over her heart. “It’s free.”

Ray barked, “But this place is falling apart!”

He was right, the ceiling split open, and pieces of crystal began raining down.

Aaron sprinted toward the shard, the crystalline, silver-red remnant of the Weave pulsing where it lay. But the moment his fingers brushed it, the chamber floor collapsed. The platform fell.

Reality bent inward. And they all plunged into darkness….

Chapter 39- The Lake That Remembers

The tunnel had spit them out onto open land. They woke one by one, as if the world itself were deciding when to let them breathe again.

Dark mud pressed against palms and cheekbones. Damp air clung to skin. The sound came first, water, endlessly patient, lapping at a shore that did not care who had survived the night. Gray morning light crept in low and cautious. No birds, no wind, just the lake.

"Where…?" Aaron rasped, struggling to open his eyes.

A warm weight pressed against him, the dragon, now back in its smaller size, wings wrapped around him protectively.

A hand touched his shoulder. Claire. "Are you hurt?" she whispered.

He shook his head. "No, I don't think so. I'm just… scared."

Claire offered a small smile. "Me too."

Ray groaned nearby, pushing himself upright. "Okay," he muttered, rubbing his head, "officially done with surprise wakeups. These old bones can't take it". Sage sat up with a gasp, clutching their graphite. Jonas was already on his feet, violin case in hand, brows furrowed.

“We fell,” Jonas said quietly. “Into something older than the arch, a pocket of the realm.”

Sage looked around. “A pocket of what?!” “A pocket of lost time,” he replied nonchalantly.

They all moved slowly, taking in their surroundings. The lake stretched before them, impossibly wide, its surface smooth as darkened glass. A light mist hovered inches above the water, never rising, never thinning. The far shore was visible, close enough to promise escape, far enough to feel unreachable. Between here and there lay the water.

No one investigated it at first; they felt it instead. A strange draw, a pull. Like standing on the edge of a cliff, and when gravity tries to pull you forward, you fight to resist.

“I don’t remember how we got here,” Ray said quietly.

“No,” answered Sage. “But I remember that we shouldn’t be……...” their voice trailing off.

Ray made the mistake of glancing down into the water. Not into the distance, but down, directly into it. The scream never finished forming.

Jonas grabbed his shoulders and yanked Ray backward as the lake answered the glance with desire. The surface rippled once, just once, and beneath it, faces. Hundreds, thousands of faces all pressed upward with mouths open in soundless pleading. Fingers scraping against the underside of the water as if it were thin ice rather than liquid. Their eyes were the worst part, not monstrous, but desperate. Endlessly desperate.

Ray fell to his knees, gasping, skin already paling as if he had seen a ghost. “What the hell…was that.”

“Don’t…,” said Jonas sharply. “Do not look again, this lake is not a place of reflection, it’s a place beyond the Weave where souls go and wait to be judged, awaiting punishment or release. Jonas explained. They did not drown here. They were placed here. And if you meet their gaze, even for a heartbeat, they will recognize something familiar in you and try to suck your soul right out of you so that they can replace it." He explained.

Ray swallowed. "Right. So. No eye contact. Got it"

A few feet down the shoreline, half-hidden in reeds bleached gray by time, rested a small wooden boat. Old, weather-worn and untied just waiting. Its oars lay inside, crossed neatly, as if someone had taken care to leave them that way.

Sage took out the graphite and knelt, their hand began to draw, "We need to get to the other side, that's where we're meant to go. I can feel it."

None of them liked how certain that felt. They stood carefully now, keeping their eyes level, fixed on the boat or the far shore, anywhere but the water. Every step closer to the lake's edge came with an ominous murmur.

Aaron could feel his heart pounding in his chest. The dragon moved even closer to his legs, almost tripping him up.

"The boat," said Ray, that's our only way. Then, quieter: "Which I hate. Just to be clear."

Up close, the wood bore marks of scratches deep claw marks. They looked like they were made by a very desperate creature.

"This isn't a rescue," Ray said. "No," Jonas agreed. "It's a passage; we need to get to the other side to move forward."

They climbed in quickly; movements practiced despite the confusion rattling through them. The boat rocked once, twice, then steadied as if it approved of their restraint. The rule was clear now, unspoken but absolute: Do not look into the lake! Do not listen to the voices! And whatever you do, do not stop rowing.

As the boat pushed off, the water stirred. The whispers grew louder, more intimate, more precise. Whispers all talking over each other," Help us, save us, I'm innocent."

Ray took the oars and dipped them in, pulling against a resistance that felt disturbingly like hands. The travelers rowed in silence, jaws clenched, eyes locked forward, each fighting battles no one else could see.

Halfway across, the mist thickened and Ray faltered. Sage took over the oars without a word. The boat veered, then corrected. Every second felt borrowed.

At last, the opposite shore loomed close, solid ground, darker mud, a rise that promised answers or at least the next kind of danger.

When the boat scraped gently against the far bank, they did not celebrate. They simply stepped out, one by one, and moved away from the water as fast as dignity allowed. Behind them, the boat drifted freely, and none of them looked back.

The lake, denied its due, fell silent once more.

Chapter 40- Jonas's Vision

The five found a level spot to regroup and decide where to go from here.

Jonas opened his violin case and began to pluck the strings…a vibration resonated.

A silver line flickered beneath his feet; he felt its pulsate and vibrate. The Weave was trying to speak.

He knelt, placed a hand upon the glowing thread, and the world vanished into his hand. His head snapped back, and the group stood silently and watched over him.

Jonas stood at the base of the Mirror Tower, spiraling upward into a sky that fractured like glass. Lightning strikes of torn time rippled overhead. The Weave hung shredded around the tower's peak, its heart exposed and bleeding silver light.

A figure stood atop the tower: Vaeron, The Unraveller. Monstrous and grand. A shape of frayed silver threads, floating like a cloak around emptiness. But the power radiating from it shook the world.

Jonas saw: Ray battling shadows and echoes of thought demons. He saw Sage drawing sigils in the air that shattered illusions. Claire was shielding the group from waves of psychic distortion, and Aaron, atop the dragon at full size, was swooping overhead. He also saw the

Weave collapsing, fiber by fiber, and the group standing on a spiraling staircase that wasn't stable. The Unraveller splits and laughs into reflections and a final decision made in fire and light. There were the possibilities of failure and rebirth. Then a final whisper: "Only love mends the center." With that, the vision shattered.

Jonas gasped, stumbling backward.
Ray caught him. "What did you see?" Ray asked.

Jonas swallowed. "The last battle at the Mirror Tower. And the world is breaking apart around it."

Aaron hugged his dragon. "Can we stop it?"

Jonas turned to face all of them, each exhausted and scared, yet united. "Yes," he said. "But only together."

Sage asked quietly, "Do we know where to go next?"

Jonas pointed to a tunnel half-hidden behind a jagged stone. It glowed faintly with silver residue.

"That way. The cave leads to the hills before the Tower."

"Then we go, we have come too far and gone through so much to stop now" Claire said.

Aaron nodded and pointed his dagger to the sky. "To fix the Weave and save the Realm."

Ray tightened his grip on his shield, Sage lifted their graphite shard, and the dragon growled low, ready for what came next.

Jonas led them into the tunnel above. The cave entrance closed softly with a large boulder as though sealing the souls in peace. Ahead, wind howled from the realm's broken horizon.

The Mirror Tower waited.

Chapter 41- Time Frays

The tunnel led them out onto open land. But it wasn't land as they knew or had seen before.

The hills rolled like frozen waves, giant stone swells frozen mid-crash. The ground was cracked with glowing red splits, as if molten breath seeped from beneath. Far off, valleys folded in on themselves in impossible geometry.

Claire stared out across the distorted horizon. "It looks like the world is… unraveling."

Jonas nodded grimly. "It is. The closer we come to the Tower, the weaker the Weave becomes."

Ray tightened his grip on the shield. "Then we move fast."

They began their trek.

The hills were steep, nearly vertical in some places, and the paths crumbled if stepped on too slowly. Sage had to draw stabilizing sigils along the way, streaking cobalt arcs across cracked earth to hold it together.

Sage panted. "We're walking across a jigsaw puzzle someone dropped on the floor."

Aaron climbed beside Ray; the dragon tucked under his arm. "Do you think everything goes back to normal when we fix the Weave?"

Ray gave him a reassuring smile. “I think life always finds a way to settle again.”

Claire added softly, “Especially when people care enough to fix what’s broken.”

Jonas said nothing; he only listened because the Weave was speaking louder now.

The wind carried faint threads of melody… and screams.

They reached the crest of the next great hill. Below lay a valley that shimmered like a heat mirage.
The trees bent into spirals, the ground thawed into liquid-reflection puddles, and shadows did not match their shapes.

Jonas held up a hand. “Wait.”

Aaron blinked. “What’s wrong?”

“It’s not real,” Jonas murmured. “Not in the way we understand.”

Claire frowned. “Another illusion?”

“The Tower is very close,” Jonas said. “Illusions will turn into attacks. Doubts into creatures and memories into traps.”

Ray snorted. “Then the illusions can try us, wouldn't be the first time something tried to use my head against me.”

But as soon as he stepped forward, he heard her voice.

Clear and soft, it was his wife’s voice. “Raymond…”

Ray froze mid-step, shield slipping.

Claire rushed to him. “Ray, it’s not her. You know it’s not her.”

The ground beneath his feet rippled, creating a shape, a woman’s silhouette, half-light, half-shadow.

Ray stepped back, knuckles white on the shield. “You’re not her,” he repeated firmly. “You’re my grief wearing her face.” The illusion broke like a wave of stone. Ray exhaled slowly, adjusting his grip on the shield. “Cheap trick,” he muttered. “Should've known better than to fall for the obvious bait.”

The valley shuddered.

Sage then cried out, gripping their head. "No, no, not this again!"

Paintings flickered in the air around them: failed art shows, critics shaking heads, blank canvases, frustrations from a thousand small failures.

"You think you're special?" the illusions whispered. "You think you matter?"

Sage screamed. Ray lunged forward, grabbing them by the shoulders. "Hey! Sage, look at me."

Their eyes were wide, terrified. Ray said firmly, "You matter to us, to all of us, and that's real."

Sage's breath steadied, and the illusions shattered like smeared ink drying too fast.

Aaron clutched the dragon close. "I don't want to see my bad futures again," he whispered. "I don't want to be that scared older me."

Claire knelt beside him. "You won't be. You're building a different path."

Jonas looked around, violin case trembling. "The Tower senses you. All of you. The stronger your spirit, the harder it pushes back."

Aaron's dragon suddenly growled a deep warning because something was forming in the valley ahead.

A mirage...A memory? No. A trap.

A glimmering staircase appeared similar to the illusion back at the Broken Arch, leading upward toward a spire-like shape that resembled the Mirror Tower.

Aaron pointed. "Is that…?"

"No," Jonas cut him off sharply. "It's a lure."

Sage narrowed their eyes. "How do we know?"

"We don't," Claire said.

Ray looked down at Aaron's dragon. "But he does."

The dragon's eyes glowed gold; it hissed at the staircase as flames sputtered from its nostrils. Then it leapt from Aaron's arms, landing at the crest of the hill. Its wings snapped open, and it blew a jet of white-blue fire straight at the staircase. The flames passed through it. The staircase flickered and twisted; it then melted into black smoke. The dragon turned to the right, toward a narrow slope hidden beneath shadowed rock. It chirped loudly.

Jonas grinned. "Of course. The Mirror Tower hides and makes its true entrance invisible. Only a creature aligned with the Weave can find it."

Ray clapped Aaron's shoulder. "Good job, kid."

Aaron blushed. "It was mostly the dragon."

They followed the dragon toward the hidden path. The trail cut between two jagged cliffs, winding downward. Fragile stone cracked beneath their feet. Wind whistled, carrying fragments of voices not their own.

Sage shivered. "This place is getting worse."

Claire nodded. "The Weave is barely holding."

Jonas's attention fixed forward, and beyond the next ridge, lightning flashed. Not in the sky, but from a tower made of mirrors, it reflected in every direction at once. They climbed the final hill and then, all five stopped.

The Mirror Tower rose from the fractured land like a broken spear plunged into the heart of the world. Its surface was made of mirrors, some cracked, some perfectly smooth, some reflecting images that didn't match reality.

Above it all, the sky bent in impossible angles, shards of light spiraling like floating glass. Threads of silver light wrapped and unwrapped around the tower's top, fraying, snapping, reforming. At the summit, there was a glow that pulsed in colors of violet, greens, and purples; it felt feral and alive.

Sage whispered, breath catching, "The source of all we have been through."

Claire’s fingers curled. “I think that’s where the Vaeron the Unraveller waits.”

Ray planted the shield tip into the ground. “And where we fix what’s broken.”

Aaron’s dragon growled low, wings flexing.

The wind howled a whisper of warning and an invitation. They took their first step toward the Mirror Tower…Together.

Chapter 42 - The Mirror Tower

The entrance to the Mirror Tower was not a door. It was a threshold of shifting reflections, the surface rippling like water touched by wind. When they stepped closer, the reflections in the glass did not keep pace with their movements.

Aaron lifted his hand, his reflection lifted a hand dripping with black tar.

Claire exhaled shakily. "The Tower already knows our fears."

Jonas placed a hand on the glass. It vibrated under his palm, humming low like the deep note of a cello. "It's alive," he whispered. "The Tower is part of the Weave… part of the Unraveller… part of all of us."

Ray braced his shield. "Alive or not, ready or not, here we go..."

The dragon stood ready next to Aaron's leg and hissed sharply, warning them but the Tower's unseen hand pushed them inside.

Light bent like a fun house effect. Gravity tilted just enough to make Aaron stumble. Wind swirled this way and that. When their eyes grew accustomed to the light, they noticed they were standing inside a vast mirrored hall. Infinite reflections. Infinite angles. Infinite them.

Sage turned slowly in place. "It's a maze."

They took one step. Then another, the floor fractured like ripples in a pond. Reflections shattered, then reformed into moving, breathing versions of themselves.

A Claire made of fractured glass stepped out of a mirror, eyes blank and cold.

A Ray whose shield dripped molten metal and a Sage whose paint-strokes dissolved into ash.

A Jonas whose violin strings were severed and bleeding black shadows, and an Aaron, the older, hollow-eyed version this time, with a crown cracked and skewed on his head, still with deep resentment in his eyes. Aaron whispered, "Oh no, not again…"

The cracked mirrored forms began to circle them. Claire reached for her younger companion.
Ray tightened his shield. Aaron's dragon growled, readying a flame.

The Aaron-reflection pointed at the real one and laughed a mocking laugh. "You're not brave," it rasped. "You're not a king. You're a scared little boy pretending to matter."

Aaron flinched. Claire stepped in front of him, trembling but firm. "That is not him." It's his fear given shape. And fear lies." Her reflection smiled coldly. "But truth hurts." Claire shuddered.

Jonas struck the ground with his bow, it sparked and drew attention. "Do not let them speak. The phantoms are loudest when you listen."

Sage inhaled, raising their graphite. "So, we silence them."

The mirror-duplicates lunged. The Ray-duplicate slammed its shield toward Ray's head, sparks exploding across metal. Ray blocked the strike, shield vibrating under the force.

Sage's duplicate hurled a streak of warped pigment, splattering the floor with a color so dark Sage felt their stomach twist.

Claire's reflection darted forward, a void of empathy hands reaching stealing, warmth, hope, breath.

Claire gasped as cold flooded her chest.

"Claire!" Aaron cried. He ran to her, but the older mirror version of himself grabbed him, hurling him backward.

Aaron crashed against the mirrored wall.

The dragon shrieked.

Aaron's reflection lifted him by the collar. "You run. You always run. You'll run now, too."

Aaron hit the floor, breath knocked out.

Ray roared, smashing his duplicate aside with a shield, a bash that cracked its glass spine.

Jonas played one harsh, discordant note. The ground quaked, forcing the phantoms to flicker.

Sage drew a symbol mid-air color spiraled outward like a comet's tail, splashing across Claire's reflection and disintegrating it.

Ray's reflection struck again, but Claire stepped forward, glowing with resolve.

"Enough!" She shouted. Her hands radiated gold. She touched Ray's reflection, and it shattered into soft light, drifting away like harmless ash.

Sage grinned, panting. "One down." Aaron staggered up. "But there are still so many."

The last reflection of Aaron's broken adult self advanced again. But this time, Aaron didn't run.

He faced it. "You're not me, I will never become you, you are weak, you pick on others," he whispered, voice shaking but sure. "I'm not alone anymore."

The dragon leapt between them, blasting a burst of shimmering fire that cracked the reflection cleanly down the middle. They began to melt like molten iron. Aaron stepped forward and pushed the pieces apart.

They dissolved. The Phantom retreated. The hall was still. But only for a breath. The Mirrors shifted, the walls slid seamlessly, clicking into new arrangements with a metallic clunk. The environment reconfigured itself, recalibrating for the next assault.

Ray cursed under his breath. "Great. It's a living puzzle box."

Jonas touched a new mirror surface. "This hall reflects intention, not reality."

Claire asked, "So how do we know which way to go?"

Sage snorted. "We don't."

Then the dragon stiffened. Its eyes glowed bright, molten gold. It stepped ahead of Aaron, skittered across the mirrored floor, and stopped at what looked like a frosted blank glass panel.

It hissed and put its forehead against the glass. The glass expanded and shifted it unfolding into an archway.

Claire gasped. "Yes! Only the guardians can see the real exits."

Jonas nodded grimly. "Because it's bound to the Weave and to Aaron."

Aaron scratched the dragon's chin gratefully. "Thank you…"

But Sage's eyes narrowed. "So, the Tower is lying again to us about where the path is."

Jonas nodded again. "The Unraveller wants us lost long before we ever reach the summit."

Ray stepped through the dragon-revealed doorway. "Then let's disappoint him."

The chamber pulsed with a vast, deliberate heartbeat *da-doom, da-doom,* each thud rolling through bone and breath alike. Above them, tendon-thick cords and shards of fractured glass hung from a ceiling lost to shadow, swaying as though the room itself were breathing. Cocooned shapes twitched faintly in the gloom, suspended between becoming and unbeing. The walls were not stone but living memory,

Translucent shapes clung to the chamber's walls and ceiling, long, eel-like forms glowing faintly crimson beneath glassy skin. They pulsed slightly out of rhythm with the great heartbeat, contracting with each *da-doom,* and advancing only in the silence between beats. When someone hesitated, even for a moment, the nearest shapes shifted closer, the air around them thickened, moments stretched thin. These were not hunters of flesh. They fed on delay, on doubt, on time that faltered, and they were very, very patient.

Obsidian flesh veined with crimson light lined the floor, which rippled subtly, glowing cracks revealing slow rivers of molten lava beneath a skin-thin surface. Footprints lingered, warm and whispering, before sealing closed. This was not a place built for trespass.

They entered the next chamber, and it was the smell that greeted them first, as the doorway behind them slammed and sealed instantly.

The smell, smelled like iron and ozone, the stale sweetness of breath trapped too long in a closed environment. Ray gagged quietly, pressing a sleeve to his nose. "Well," he muttered, voice thin, "good news is we're definitely not early. This place has been… marinating." He glanced back at the others, then added, "And I should know, I collect trash for a living." The chamber opened before them, ribbed high above like the inside of a vast chest, red light seeping between its struts in time with the distant *da-doom*. Fibrous strands hung from the ceiling, tightening and relaxing as if breathing, while the floor sloped inward, dark and glassy, beneath their feet. Ray took one careful step, then froze as the ground seemed to cling before releasing him. "I would like to formally request," he finished, swallowing, "that whatever's in charge of time down here please stop touching my ankles."

Chapter 43- The Spiraling Platforms

The golden staircase spiraled downward into a vast cylindrical shaft, but unlike the reflective halls above, this space felt organic, almost vascular. Threads of silver, gold, and copper wove along the walls in slow, pulsing currents, like living veins carrying strained light instead of blood. The air was warm, faintly humming, each breath carrying a sense of change rather than decay.

Jonas slowed as they descended, his voice barely above a whisper. "We are inside the Weave's root."

Claire reached out, fingertips brushing the wall. It recoiled gently in pulsating reflex, like living tissue startled from sleep.

Ray lifted his shield, eyes scanning. "Okay," he muttered, "that officially confirms we're not trespassing, we're inside someone's nervous system."

Sage's brow furrowed. "It's alive."

Aaron hugged the dragon close. "The Tower feels… scared, or maybe that's just me."

Jonas nodded. “The Weave is collapsing, but it’s still trying to function. The Tower isn’t trapping us anymore.”

Claire glanced back up at the entrance, the light above dimming. “…It’s trying to warn us.”

The dragon growled low, a sound that vibrated through the threads around them. Its wings flared, fire flickering between its teeth.

“What is it?” Aaron asked. Jonas narrowed his eyes. “It smells the distortion. Illusion.”

The corridor ended abruptly, opening into a colossal chamber formed from intersecting threads of light and matter. Dozens of paths stretched outward with bridges, stairs, floating platforms, impossible walkways twisting in gravity-defying spirals. The chamber felt tense, overloaded, like a mind flooded with too many thoughts at once.

Sage exhaled slowly. “None of those can be real.”

Jonas nodded. “Correct. The Weave is misfiring. The Unraveller is throwing possibilities at us, hoping one makes us stop.”

Aaron swallowed. “I bet Dragon can show us again which one is real?”

The dragon walked out ahead, nose low, sniffing the air. It padded to the nearest stone bridge,
blasted it with a jet of white-blue flame, and the bridge dissolved into smoke.

Ray let out a breathy laugh. “Efficient.” The dragon moved again and repeated, path, flame, dissolve, path, flame, dissolve.

Claire watched closely. “It’s not destroying the Weave,” she said softly. “It’s clearing the noise.”

Finally, at the very edge of the chamber, the dragon stopped before a simple, dimly lit stone walkway. It sniffed. Waited. Nothing happened. No resistance. No illusion.

Sage blinked. "Is it… safe?"

Jonas nodded. "It's real."

Ray stepped onto the walkway first, testing the stone. Solid, then Claire followed, then Sage, Aaron, and the dragon, with Jonas last, bow raised.

The moment they were across, the chamber failed, like a system pushed beyond its limit; it collapsed into nothingness.

Pathways fractured. Platforms spiraled into darkness. Threads stretched too far finally gave way, the Tower convulsing with the strain of a world trying to hold itself together and failing.

Ray swore under his breath. "We have to move!" They ran.

The walkway bucked beneath them, reality tilting. Veins of light flickered wildly, sparks bursting like exhausted stars.

"It's unraveling too fast!" Sage cried. "We will… make it," Claire insisted, pain etched across her face.

The Weave itself spasmed. Space folded. Direction lost meaning. One moment downhill, then sideways, then wrong entirely.

Aaron stumbled. Ray scooped him up without breaking stride.

Claire thrust her hands outward. Warm light bloomed, steady and calm. The air smoothed. The floor steadied, responding and relieved, as though grateful for the help.

Jonas listened, jaw tight. "The Tower is thinning… the distortions are desperate."

Walls split open, revealing alternate versions of the group running different paths, trapped in looping failures.

Echo-Ray pounded invisible walls, Echo-Sage ran in circles, sobbing, Echo-Claire lay motionless, and Echo-Aaron curled around a tiny dragon skeleton.

Claire gasped. “They’re not real, right?”

“They were possible,” Jonas said quietly. “Outcomes the Weave is showing us, hoping fear will turn us back.”

Sage turned away, trembling. “Please… stop…”

“Eyes forward, just keep moving!” Jonas snapped.

The dragon screeched and unleashed a furious blast of flame. The false visions evaporated.

Aaron hugged it tight. “Good job… good job buddy.”

The walkway narrowed into a spiraling descent. Below them, the Weave pulsed brighter, urgently.

“We’re close,” Jonas said. “Very close.”

They descended into the final chamber. The stairs ended in an arena-like hollow. Above them, the Tower stretched endlessly upward. Below, a vortex of silver threads churned slowly, frayed, uneven, dimming like a star in its last moments.

The air here was quiet. Empty as if in mourning.

Threads drifted loose, severed ends dissolving into nothing. Whole sections of the Weave were simply gone, leaving gaps that hurt to look at, an absence where structure should have been.

Sage’s voice broke. “It’s already been tearing itself apart…”

Jonas nodded grimly. “This isn’t a battle we’re preventing; it’s a funeral we’re interrupting,”

At the center stood a single mirrored archway, cracked down the middle. Its surface flickered weakly, symbols barely holding their shape.

Claire stepped forward, eyes shining. “It’s still here,” she whispered. “After everything… It’s still trying.”

The dragon lowered its head, a low murmuring sound escaping its throat.

The Weave pulsed once more, faintly yet determined, and very much afraid. And in that moment, they understood. They weren’t just fighting the Unraveller. They were standing in the aftermath of its cruelty.

And whatever lay beyond the archway had already cost the world dearly. Claire drew a steady breath. “A moment more,” she said. “Then this ends.”

Ray rested his shield against the stone. “Together is the only way.”

Jonas nodded. “Always.”

Sage straightened. “For what’s left.”

Aaron swallowed, stroking the dragon’s neck. “I hope it can still be saved.”

Jonas placed his hand on the archway.

“Prepare yourselves,” he said quietly. “The next step… is the beginning of the end.”

Chapter 44 – The Echo of the Unraveller

The next chamber was long and narrow, lined entirely with reflective walls, but these mirrors were not still; they moved. Each reflection lags half a second behind the real movement of the group. When Ray lifted his shield, his reflection lifted it late. When Aaron blinked, his reflection blinked twice. Claire's reflection cracked at the edges as if something inside the mirror was pushing outward.

Jonas frowned. "The Tower is unstable. Its illusions are blurring into the real."

Sage swallowed. "Meaning?"

"Meaning," Claire said softly, "if we aren't careful, we might lose track of which part is the illusion and which is us."

They walked slowly. Each step echoed in ways that didn't match the sound of their boots. Reflections leaned inches too close or looked over their shoulders before they did. Aaron's dragon hissed at every surface, tail lashing. Then the ceiling shifted and their reflections multiplied into dozens of images. It reflected every angle of themselves, every fear, and every version that almost was. The illusions whispered: "Turn back…, You'll fail…, The Weave dies with you…, Why fight what's already broken?"

Ray slammed his shield against the wall, shattering a mirror. He glanced at the mess and said, "Oops," with a rueful half-smile as the mirror reformed instantly.

Jonas stepped up beside him. "We can't break our way out. The Tower is feeding off our strength."

Aaron tugged on Claire's sleeve. "I think it's getting stronger."

Claire nodded. "Yes, and more desperate."

The reflection staring back at Sage wasn't Sage exactly. It was a twisted version, all hunched, face smeared with ink, eyes hollow, fingers dripping pigment as if they'd tried to paint themselves out of existence. Sage took a step back. "I'm glad that's not me." But the reflection smiled and reached out of the mirror. The hand that emerged was made of liquid ink that hardened into claws.

Ray immediately leapt between Sage and the creature, shield raised. "Back off, wet spot!"

More reflections poured from the mirrors. Shadow-Claire with hollow eyes, the Shadow-Ray with a broken shield, the Shadow-Jonas with strings like barbed wire, and the Shadow-Aaron wearing a broken, dull crown. The Tower was spawning distortions of their worst selves.

Aaron cried out. "They look real!"

"They are real," Jonas said sharply, drawing his bow. "Illusions given form by the Tower's unraveling."

Claire raised her hands, the glow brightening in her palms. "They're manifestations of our very real pain and fear!"

Ray braced the shield at the ready. "Then we treat them like any other threat."

The ink-Sage creature lunged, but Ray blocked it. Jonas struck a vibrating note that staggered the others. Claire infused the air with

warm energy that pushed back the distorted Claire-reflection.
Aaron ducked under a swipe from the crown-wearing reflection of himself.

Sage, shaking, finally raised their graphite shard. “ENOUGH!” They slammed the graphite against the ground.

Color exploded outward, swirling in hues of violet, blue, and sunrise gold, washing over the reflections and pulling their shape apart. The ink forms dissolved into pigment dust and drifted upward into the mirrors, sealing them temporarily.

Aaron breathed hard. “Is it over?”

Jonas shook his head slowly. “No. I think the Tower’s illusions were just warming up.”

The dragon suddenly screeched a high and urgent shriek.

All of them turned. One of the mirrors was glowing gold. Not distorted black, they had become used to but gold.

The dragon ran to it, scratching the surface. The gold rippled like a pool of molten metal.

A passage appeared. But unlike the previous illusion-stairs, the dragon stepped onto these rungs, and the step held.

Jonas whispered, “A path downward…”

Claire blinked. “Not upward? The Tower’s summit is above.”

“No,” Jonas said firmly. “The true heart of the Tower is below. The Unraveller hides beneath the roots of the Weave.”

Ray nodded once. “Then we go down.” He lifted his shield; Sage drew a steady breath.
Claire squeezed Aaron’s hand. And Jonas tucked his violin under his chin.

They stepped into the passage, and a shockwave pulsed through the hallway. The mirrors darkened, their reflections blown out like candles. The gold staircase flickered.

Ray growled, "Hold the path open!"

Sage slammed their graphite against the door threshold and the pigment flowed, stabilizing the gold.

Then the mirrors began to shatter inward as if something on the other side was breaking through.

A thin silhouette stepped out of the broken corridor, shimmering with black-and-silver threads waving like smoke. The shape had no face, no clear edges, trailing behind it was a cloak of unraveling fibers.

Claire's breath hitched. "It's… hollow."

Jonas's eyes narrowed. "It's just a shadow, a projection of the real thing."

The creature glided toward them without touching the ground. The air thickened. Its presence pulled threads of reality loose, the walls bent toward it, and all the reflections warped.

Ray stepped in front. "Stay behind me."

The creature spoke without making a sound, using telepathy, that everyone heard exactly what it was saying inside their heads and in their bones.

"TURN BACK. ALL THREADS BREAK. YOU CANNOT MEND WHAT LONGS TO END."

Aaron shook violently. "It's in my head."

Claire grabbed his hand. "Ignore it!"

The dragon roared, making blue flames spiral upward.

The creature flicked a finger, and time slowed. The flame froze in midair.

Aaron's breath caught.

Sage gasped. "It's controlling time!"

Jonas stepped forward. He lifted his violin and played a note that broke time's grip.

The world snapped back. Into place. The creature twisted toward Jonas.

"YOU, SONGWEAVER, YOU SEE THE PATTERN."

Jonas's jaw clenched. "And I'll see it restored."

The creature reached for him with a hand of unraveling threads.

Ray slammed it with his shield. The impact caught the creature by surprise, sending it staggering backwards.

Claire placed both palms on the ground, and a warm gold light flared, pushing back the hollow creature further.

Sage painted a sigil in gold and cobalt that anchored the passage.

Aaron's dragon grew larger, flames enveloping its body.

Aaron stepped forward, voice trembling but firm: "You can't stop us; we stand together."

The creature shrieked, form fracturing at the edges.

Jonas played a rising chord. Claire's light expanded. Ray held the front. Sage sealed the cracks.

The dragon unleashed a white-blue fire that collided with the creature and the creature exploded into threads of shadow that dissolved into nothing.

Silence fell. The gold staircase solidified completely.

Jonas lowered his violin. "We go now!"

Ray nodded.
Sage and Claire steadied themselves, and Aaron and the dragon flew out above them, tail flicking.

Together, they scurried downward into the heart of the Tower, toward the Unraveller.

Toward the end.

Chapter 45 – The Descent Through Unmaking

The passage did not open on a floor; it ended abruptly in open space.

Beyond the edge drifted a scatter of pale stone platforms suspended in a vast interior hollow of the Tower, like fragments of a shattered path slowly orbiting one another. Some hovered close. Others drifted far below. They slid, stalled, rotated, then reversed direction, each moving according to a rhythm that did not repeat. They did not behave like steps. They behaved like hesitations.

Ray stopped short. “Those aren’t steps. Those are… opportunities to die.”

Behind them, footprints pressed into the dust of the final step. Then another, then another. They continued forward off the edge, into nothing, forming perfect impressions in open air before appearing on the nearest floating slab. Something unseen was already crossing. The prints deepened. Faint silver light pooled within them. Then they lifted, unraveling upward like smoke.

Sage whispered, “Something’s here.”

Jonas’s voice was quiet. “The Tower can no longer finish the things it makes. Only their effects.”

One of the drifting slabs eased closer, turning slowly as though an invitation. Waiting.

The dragon flew close to Aaron and chirped with encouragement, "I think it wants us to cross using the moving platforms." Aaron stepped back one step, then jumped…. For a breath, he hung above the void, then the stone beneath him hardened. A strange, toneless vibration passed through the air, felt more than heard.

"It only stabilizes when something living commits," Jonas said. "And only briefly."

Already, the edges of the platform were softening, dust lifting from them like steam.

"It won't hold," Ray said.

Aaron took another step backwards, then jumped again.

The first platform immediately began to shed itself into glittering grit.

"Let's move!" Jonas encourages. They ran, jumped, and landed, stabilized, and then did it again, each following a different path. Each jump was a decision the Tower barely honored.

The space around them bent strangely. Nearby slabs burned with flame that flowed like water. Others glistened with frost that radiated heat. One rang like struck crystal when Ray landed. Another swallowed Sage's boot an inch too deep before stiffening again.

Claire jumped, light flaring from her palms, but it spilled sideways, briefly outlining vast invisible forms drifting near the platforms. Her glow curved around nothing.

Something enormous shifted. A series of massive impressions pressed into the dust of a distant slab before slowly lifting away.

Ray swore. "Whatever that was, it wasn't friendly."

“It wasn’t hostile,” Jonas said. “It didn’t notice us.”

Aaron’s chest tightened. A certainty crept over him that he had already failed something. That the next jump would only prove it.

The dragon chirped encouragingly the feeling loosened.

They were running out of stones. The remaining platforms jittered now, sliding in shallow, broken arcs.

Aaron jumped once more, and the platform he launched from let go.

His foot met nothing. The world dropped away.

Wind tore the breath from his chest as the void opened beneath him, vast and soundless. Far below, the silver turbulence of the Weave’s heart swelled, as though noticing him.

“Aaron!” Claire cried.

For a weightless heartbeat, he fell through a place where up and down had not yet been decided. Then…Heat, claws locked into his coat.

The dragon shrieked and erupted into full flight, wings spreading open with a violent flare of molten light. Fire blasted backward, diving, forcing the air itself to behave.

The fall wrenched sideways, Aaron slammed against scaled warmth, arms locking instinctively around the dragon’s neck as it beat once, twice, muscles shuddering under impossible strain. The invisible presence recoiled.

The dragon climbed. It threw them with a final explosive wingbeat that hurled them toward the nearest drifting slab.

Claire’s light lashed outward. The platform seized solidity.

Aaron and the dragon struck hard, skidding across the surface. The stone cracked like ice under sudden weight.

The dragon collapsed around him, wings wrapped tight, chest heaving, sweat bleeding through his clothes, and for a moment, Aaron could not breathe. Then he felt it, the frantic hammer of the dragon's heart. He pressed his face into its neck. "You saved me…"

The dragon chirped weakly and nudged him, smoke leaking from its nostrils.

Ray gave an awkward and uncomfortable laugh, sharp and shaking. "Great. Perfect. My least favorite thing. Watching kids fall into cosmic nothing." Then he tightened his grip on the shield. "After this, I'm walking on flat ground for the rest of my life. I don't care where the war is."

Jonas met his eyes. "Then let's earn you that ground."

The dragon crouched and launched again.

They followed. The void pressed inward. The air folded. Footprints bloomed across the final stones all at once, this time just standing, waiting.

The platforms began to dim.

"The Tower can't hold both," Jonas said. "Us and whatever that is."

They moved and jumped onto the last platform.

Aaron leapt with the dragon.

Jonas jumped last, for a breath, and he was nowhere.

Then the final slab caught him and slid into alignment with a broad, stable platform of dark, solid stone. Ahead, the world sharpened the contradictions thinned. Fire burned upward again.

They stood at the edge of a vast circular hollow carved from dark, unadorned material. Above, the Tower's interior rose as a distant ring stripped of ornament. Below, the Weave's heart strained with silver currents folding over one another like a shiny object seen through deep water. At its center stood a single marbled arch.

Sage whispered, “That’s it.”

Jonas nodded. “The final door. The last place the Tower still remembers clearly.”

Aaron looked up. Along the fractured center, faint symbols guttered into being, their marks and between them, the wounded spiral.

“That’s us,” he said softly. Jonas stepped forward and placed his hand on the arch. It was cold.

It did not resist. “Prepare yourselves, take a breath,” he said. “The next step isn’t a descent, it’s an ending.”

Chapter 46 – The Heart of Unmaking

The Dragon breathed a blue-grey ball of Dragon breath into the arch. It cracked and split open with a sound like tearing fabric. Light poured out, unnatural light. A cold, crystalline radiance, sharp as the sun reflecting off ice, engulfed them.

When it faded, they stood in a vast chamber suspended in nothingness. No walls and a floor they could not see. There was only a platform made of interwoven silver threads, impossibly delicate like fragile snowflakes, the very heart of the Weave floating in an abyss of fractured reflections.

Above them, the sky wasn't sky at all but a dome of swirling glass crystal fragments, each reflecting a different version of reality. Some fragments gleamed clear and bright, others had gone dark, their surfaces cracked and threatening to disintegrate.

Claire whispered: "It's beautiful."

At the far end of the platform stood a figure. Not hidden, not even trying to disguise itself. Vaeron The Unraveller. It wasn't monstrous, unlike the distorted guardians. I did not look like an echo or an avatar.

The Unraveller's form was small, almost feeble looking, a smooth shell of shifting threads surrounding an empty center. Its body flickered between humanoid insect-like and shapeless cloud, unable to hold a single identity. It was childlike in size; its frame wrapped in unraveling strands of reality. An empty nothingness where something should be.

Aaron whispered, "…It's tiny."

Sage swallowed. "Don't let that fool you."

The Unraveller's head tilted. It had no face, but they felt its attention.

Jonas spoke gently, carefully. "Why are you doing this?"

The Unraveller's voice filled the chamber not with sound, but a deep vibration that rattled bone.

"I END BECAUSE ENDING IS THE FINAL HONESTY."

Claire stepped forward, golden light flickering across her hands. "There is pain in the Weave. I know. But destruction won't heal it."

"HEALING IS A LIE. ALL THREADS BREAK. ALL STORIES END. ALL HOPE FADES."

Ray braced himself. "We're here to make sure they don't."

The Unraveller turned toward him. Threads whipped out, skimming his shield.

Ray stumbled as the pressure made the metal warp at the slightest touch.

Claire grabbed his shoulder. "Are you okay?"

Ray nodded. "It's stronger than it looks."

Jonas exhaled. "This is the real fight now."

Aaron's dragon, perched behind him in full size, tried to leap, but its feet had been absorbed into the floor with slick black ropes. The Unraveller didn't move. It simply unmade the floor beneath them. The Weave platform cracked like glass. Segments fell away into the abyss and were swallowed instantly.

Ray roared, throwing his shield outward to anchor them. The ruby glowed, threads snapping into place and holding the platform together.

Sage shouted, "It's tearing the Weave apart!"

"YOUR GIFTS WERE STOLEN FROM A BROKEN WORLD," the Unraveller intoned.
"RETURN THEM TO THE ZERO."

The Unraveller raised its tentacle, and mirror-duplicates burst from the sky, dozens of them, each carrying twisted versions of the Five's gifts.

Fire without warmth.
Light without life.
Ink without creation.
Sound without harmony.
Protection without purpose.

They swarmed the platform. Ray stepped forward, shield blazing with protective runes.
"Get behind me!"

The first wave of duplicates crashed against him. His shield flared, absorbing the echoes, redirecting force, holding the line.

Claire placed her palms on the ground. Golden warmth radiated outward, stabilizing chunks of the platform so Ray had footing.

Sage swung their graphite, painting sigils in the air. Each symbol became a shape, a barrier, binding into solid dark lines, driving back ink-drenched copies.

Jonas's violin case snapped open by itself. The violin floated into his hands. He began to play. Notes spiraled outward like silver ribbons, striking mirror-duplicates and unraveling them into harmless dust. His melody held the fragments of the Weave together.

And Aaron…Aaron stood trembling behind Ray, but he had his dagger in hand, ready to stand tall when needed, the dragon roaring beside him.

The duplicates pressed closer. The boy tightened his grip around the Griffin claw. "I'm not afraid of you," he whispered to the illusions.

The dragon crouched low, fire building in its chest.

Jonas shouted over the chaos: "Aaron! You and the guardian must focus on the core! The Unraveller is channeling through the copies. Break its control!"

Aaron nodded, eyes filled with determination beyond his years. He knelt and, using his dagger, sliced through the tethers holding the Dragon in place. He pointed at the Unraveller.

Aaron mounted the dragon, holding tight around its neck. They launched into the air a streak of molten gold.

The Unraveller lifted its thread-like fingers. The dragon froze mid-flight, caught in another web of unraveling strands. Aaron screamed, "NO!" he slid further down the dragon's spine and began cutting the cords. The blade, sharp and true, made easy work of the threads as well.

Jonas's bow split in two, then reshaped, creating a sharper, harder sound capable of piercing the strands. He played a note so powerful that the chamber vibrated and undid the remaining threads

The Unraveller flinched.

The dragon and Aaron tumbled free, the dragon catching itself midair.

Claire surged forward, white light erupting from her like a ball of blazing sun.
Her glow struck the nearest mirror-duplicates, calming the degraded energy fueling them.

Ray's shield expanded, absorbing a massive blast from a duplicate-cluster.

Sage's graphite spun in a circle of pulsing colors, trapping several more illusions inside a painted ring.

Jonas pointed his bow-tip at the Unraveller. "It's weakening. It's pulling from the illusions to sustain itself."

Sage realized it, too. "If we break the illusions, we break it."

Claire's voice rose. "And if we stand together, it can't unravel us."

Ray slammed forward, clearing a path. Aaron's dragon rose again.
Jonas played louder,
Sage painted faster, and Claire shone brighter.

And the Weave beneath them, for the first time in ages, pulsed with hope.

Chapter 47 – The Shattering of the Tower

The mirror-duplicates shattered one by one, dissolving into drifting fragments of melted thread as the Five fought in unison. With every duplicate destroyed, the Unraveller's form flickered, its shape stuttering, its hollow center pulsing.

Claire saw it first. "It's weakening…I think"

The Unraveller convulsed. Its fragile, childlike silhouette imploded, threads coiling, knotting, tightening, and then it burst outward in a storm of unraveling fibers, dust, and strands.

A new form rose taller, stretching into a towering figure of blackness, a wound in reality that bled darkness instead of blood. Its towering and vast form seemed to occupy more space than the room could contain, its edges blurring into non-existence. Where it moved, light didn't merely dim: it was totally absorbed.

Shadows pooled around its form like spilled black ink, spreading across the floor and walls with deliberate malevolence, and where those shadows touched, color drained away as though being digested. The very idea of light seemed to offend it. Torches guttered and died. Lanterns imploded.

The worst part was the silence it carried, not just an absence of sound, but something more profound. It was as though the creature moved through a bubble of absolute absence, where even echoes did not exist.

Aaron. "Okay, that's bad."

Jonas corrected softly. "Yes, seems hungry and desperate."

The Unraveller molded itself a head of shifting emptiness, and the chamber squealed. A voice of undeniable dread came from the Unraveller: "YOU DEFY THE END.
YOU REFUSE PEACE, YOU ARE NOTHING BUT DELAY."

The Tower vibrated. Cracks appeared in the crystal dome above a long, jagged lightning strike across the sky seemed to break time for a second.

Ray braced himself. "Then we'll delay you forever." He swallowed hard, "I can't believe I just said that."

The Unraveller's black newly formed tentacles extended, splitting into a thousand threads like a Man of War jellyfish, aiming to suck their souls from their bodies.

Claire ran forward, glowing brighter than ever. Her light intercepted the tentacles
But they wrapped around her wrists, pulling her toward the void.

She screamed as the barbs pierced her skin. She held her ground "I…won't…let…you…take…ANYTHING!"

Her aura exploded in beams of shimmering iridescent light, forcing the threads to recoil.

Aaron rushed to her side. "Claire!"

"I'm okay, go! Help the others!"

Aaron nodded, choking back fear.

The battle had only truly begun.

The Weave-platform tilted under them as cracks split through it, threads snapping as strings pulled too tight.

Jonas shouted over the roaring chaos, "The Tower's core is destabilizing! If we don't end this soon…"

Sage finished grimly, "…there won't be a Tower or a Weave left to save."

Above, giant slabs of mirror broke away and fell like meteors.

Ray lifted his shield, catching a falling shard and shattering it with a guttural roar.
Claire shielded Aaron and the dragon with an extended aura from a spray of glass.
Jonas played an urgent chord that redirected falling debris.
And Sage painted a floating barrier of intertwined pigments that caught fragments midair.

Still, the Tower was disintegrating. And the Unraveller fed on the destruction.

It inhaled, and the cracks deepened. It exhaled and time warped, slowing, speeding, distorting around them.

Aaron cried out as a time-ripple nearly froze him mid-step, but Jonas struck the ground with his bow.

"Move, Aaron! Stay close!"

The boy obeyed, and the dragon pushed him behind Ray.

The Unraveller raised both arms, and a whirlwind of broken reflections spun around it.

"ALL THREADS RETURN TO THE VOID."

"Nope, not today," Ray snarled. He slammed the shield into the ground. "You want them, you have to go through me!"

The ruby flared, sending a shockwave of shimmering red energy outward. Every unraveling thread that touched it dissolved into harmless dust. He roared with the effort, becoming the immovable wall between the Unraveller and the others.

The platform steadied.

Jonas shouted, voice cracking, "Ray! You're anchoring the Weave!"

Ray grinned through the strain. "About time I pulled my weight."

Sage stepped forward, graphite raised. Their eyes glowed with raw creative force.

They began painting in midair, symbols, strokes, spirals, and geometric glyphs, each stroke becoming a barrier, an assault, or a reweaving of damaged thread. Their pigments pierced the edges of nothingness like spears of colored light. Sage cried out, "I create with love and truth!" The Tower shuddered as their art rewove broken pieces back together.

Jonas began to play a melody. The notes rose and fell in a pattern older than time itself.

The air vibrated, and the unraveling slowed even further. The Tower's collapse paused, and even the Unraveller twitched, threads faltering in rhythm.

Jonas's voice joined the music: "Hold together… hold, hold…!"

The dragon roared in harmony, amplifying each note. Claire moved with impossible grace, weaving between Ray, Sage, and the falling debris. Her hands glowed with pure light, touching broken Weave-threads and mending them as fast as the Unraveller tore them apart. She confronted a wave of void-thread rushing straight for Aaron.

Claire stepped into it. Her glow exploded outward, creating a dome of peace that quelled the assault. Her voice was soft, but firm. "You don't run from the dark; you have to face it head-on."

The void curled from her warmth like frost melting. Aaron finally stepped forward, his arrowhead symbol glowed on his chest. His dagger in his hand, his eyes burned with fierce determination.

The dragon inhaled, gathering a roaring sphere of white-blue fire in his torso. Aaron pointed at the Unraveller.

"Now! Dragon, he weakened - let's go."

The dragon launched the fire straight into the Unraveller's hollow core and the chamber exploded with light. The explosion ripped threads from the Unraveller's form. It screamed the sound of a dying universe. Its towering frame flickered, shrinking slightly.

Jonas gasped. "That hurt it, now's your chance!"

Sage nodded. "Aaron, do it again! Your fire reaches the place we can't!"

The boy nodded fiercely. The dragon inhaled again.

Claire steadied the Weave beneath them.

Ray held the line.

Jonas steadied time with music.

Sage painted sigils channeling the fire into a focused strike.

Aaron shouted, "All for one and five for all!" his voice rang out, impossible to ignore.

And the dragon released a second blast directly into the heart of the Unraveller.

The Tower cracked and the Weave glowed, the Unraveller shrieked and doubled over, looking as if it was absorbing itself into itself, the chamber itself shook violently.

Everything was accelerating toward the end.

Chapter 48 – The Love That Defied the Void

But then… just as the five thought it was over…. Vaeron inhaled and erupted outward in a new form. A monstrous vortex of unraveling threads towered above them, stretching from platform to broken sky. Arms like enormous whips lashed from its body. A ribcage of shattered remains expanded and contracted with each hollow breath. At its center spun the void bottomless, ravenous, widening.

Light, sound, color, and hope. The air began to spin in a vortex of mirrors, shadows, echo and glass. Everything in the chamber dimmed as the Unraveller pulled it inward, sucking it all in like a gigantic vacuum cleaner…The creature screeched a sound so high and sharp it split mirrors above them.

Ray groaned, shield shaking. Oh no, here we go again."

Sage whispered, trembling, "It can't hold a shape anymore. It's everything and nothing."

Jonas looked grim. This is its true state: the pure desire to end everything."

The Unraveller raised a limb made up of twisting threads. Time folded, and the weave buckled one last time. And then the entire structure began to collapse. The crystal dome overhead shattered into a thousand falling fragments, each reflecting a different, impossible version of the world that they knew. Famine, sadness, pain, there was no color left, only grey skies and grey desert sand, no warmth, no music, and no love. The weave that held it all in place was no longer.

Ray raised the shield above them, forming a canopy. The reflective crystal shards slammed into it, bouncing away harmlessly.

The Weave-platform beneath them frayed at the edges, silver threads unraveling into the void. Sage sprinted to the nearest breaking point, graphite painting repairs as fast as possible.

Jonas struck a violent chord, and time slowed just enough for the group to avoid being crushed by a falling slab of Tower wall.

The Unraveller lifted both arms. "THE END IS THE ONLY WAY YOU CREATE A NEW WEAVE, ONE THAT I CHOOSE TO CREATE."

Its voicc rippled through the chaos. The platform tilted sharply, nearly throwing them into the abyss.

Claire shouted, "We can't win by force!"

Ray snarled, "Then what do we do?!"

Claire understood. That they had reached the point were strength, art, music, protection, flame, none of it alone could win. Only the things that had grown between them from the Red Door to now, "The only way you dispel darkness, you have to be the light in it, the opposite of darkness is love, unity, connection, and trust," she said.

Claire stepped forward first, hands glowing warm gold. "We face despair with compassion." Ray stepped beside her, shield braced. "We face destruction with protection." Sage joined them, graphite blazing with multi-colored light. "We face nothingness with creation." Jonas lifted his violin, bow trembling. "We face silence with harmony." And Aaron took a breath, standing before the enormous dragon whose wings wrapped around them like sheltering branches. "And we face fear with courage." The dragon roared in resonance with their unity.

The Unraveller lashed toward them. A tidal wave of unraveling void washed forward. The Five stepped together, each standing shoulder to shoulder. A single circuit. A single connection.

Jonas whispered the truth he had sensed since the beginning: "This is how the Weave heals."

Light beamed from them in a tidal wave of colors and sound. the pure spectrum of life and meaning. It collided with the Unraveller's devastating attack. Void met unity, nothing met everything, and death met love. And for the first time…

The Unraveller recoiled; it screamed, but this time in fear. Its form began to crack, threads unraveling at impossible speed. The void did not explode or fall or scatter. It simply stopped being. The ash that remained hung in the air for one crystalline moment before dissolving into nothing, leaving only a strange perfect silence.

Claire gasped, realization hitting her like a heartbeat. It was done!

Ray growled, "Good., I know exactly how to take the trash out."

Then the ground beneath their feet began to vibrate. Aaron gulped, "It's still…." But before he could get the words out, the Weave ignited. Threads shot outward like veins of living starlight. The entire realm pulsed with breath, expanding and contracting like a newborn world drawing its first air.

The shattered mirrors reformed into a vast dome of unbreakable clarity. The Tower's walls healed, harmonious. The abyss filled with woven light, and the broken archways rewrote themselves.

The realm was being reborn under their feet; the platform of threads rewove itself in spiraling patterns.

Sage looked upward, tears slipping down their cheeks. "It's... magnificent."

Ray exhaled deeply, heaving his chest with exhaustion and relief. "I think we actually did it."

Jonas's violin played a soft, involuntary note of awe. "The Weave... it's singing again."

Claire stepped forward, hands trembling. She touched the growing thread; the Weave felt alive, warm, and peaceful. She whispered, "I've never felt such love."

A voice rang out of the ethos: - Thank you, Thread bearers. And with that, a wave of warmth touched each of them.

Aaron felt the dragon press its head to him one last time. "Are you... leaving?" he whispered. The Dragon, now small again, closed its eyes, and in the gleaming surface of his bronze scales, Aaron saw not a goodbye but gratitude and a newfound bond. He wrapped his arms tightly around the dragon's neck, as if holding on could keep this moment from ending.

Aaron wiped his eyes. "Goodbye, friend." Then the dragon dissolved into pure, golden fire, and that flame flew upward into the Weave where it rejoined the guardian threads.

Claire pulled him into a warm embrace. "You'll see it again someday. All guardians return."

Jonas closed the violin case. "The Weave is whole. Our task is complete."

The realm shimmered, and the light around them bent gently inward......forming a portal.

The stone circle. Their way home. They stepped out into morning light.

Not the morning they had left behind, but one that felt newly made of softer light, the air felt clearer, the world breathing evenly again.

They stood within the stone circle. The work was done.

Beyond the stones, the land stretched wide and whole. Hills rolled gently toward the horizon. Forest canopies no longer twisted inward but reached for the sun. Even the wind sounded different, no longer strained, no longer searching, the Seas and sea life all flowing in rhythm and brimming with the bounty of life.

Aaron turned slowly in place. “Did we… fix it?”

Jonas smiled, tired but content. “Yes, and we reminded it how to hold itself together.”

Ray exhaled deeply, a sound he hadn’t realized he’d been holding in. “That’ll do.”

Claire closed her eyes. For the first time in years, the weight inside her chest was gone. She breathed in, slow and steady, and felt herself present in her own body.

Sage knelt, touching the stone beneath their fingertips. The lines here were complete. No distortion. No wandering charcoal paths. “It’s quiet,” they said.

“Yes,” Morwyn’s voice answered. She stood at the edge of the circle, shawl wrapped around her shoulders, eyes bright with relief and something like pride.

“You did well, Thread-bearers,” she said simply.

Jonas inclined his head. “We had help.”

Morwyn smiled at the group, then looked beyond them.

The Red Door stood once more at the far edge of the clearing. It was closed. The paint no longer peeled. The color was deep and settled. The knocker hung straight, no longer askew.

Aaron hesitated. "Does that mean… It's over?"

Morwyn considered this. "Yes, for now."

Jonas added gently, "There will always be a greedy, hateful someone wanting to rule the world, so the door will call again when it's needed."

One by one, they felt the gentle pull of their own lives calling them back.

Ray adjusted his gloves. Sage tucked graphite into their pouch. Claire straightened her coat, steady and sure. Aaron tucked his hands into his pockets.

Jonas lingered a moment longer, listening to the silence settle into its proper shape. Then he turned, violin case tapping lightly at his side.

The stone circle faded behind them as they walked away

The Red Door remained; it stood watch in the middle of an otherwise blank wall surrounded by a slouching row of buildings and a coffee shop on the corner that always smelled like cinnamon and honey.

Epilogues

Claire

Claire sat in the quiet break room of Crescent Clinic, a cup of tea warming her palms. For the first time in years, she felt light. As if all the heaviness she had carried for so long had finally found somewhere to rest.

She moved differently now. When she sat at a bedside, the fear no longer clung skin. She let it pass through her, named it, softened it, and released it. She learned how to set the weight down at the end of each shift, how to breathe without bracing herself for grief. She understood that life and death happen just as they are meant to, and all she could do was help remove any fear.

Patients noticed too. They said she had a calming presence. That time seemed to slow, and pain eased when she spoke or touched them. Even the worst moments felt less sharp.

Claire just smiled a knowing smile. She understood now. The gift she had run from her whole life was not a burden. They were a bridge.

Sometimes, when a life slipped gently from the world, she felt Kaelith nearby as a reassurance, steady and quiet.

And when she sat looking at the Red Door from the familiar bus stop, she would touch the double-hand pendant around her neck with fond memories; she no longer wondered what was behind it. She knew.

Aaron

Aaron walked to school the way he always did, his backpack bouncing, shoes scuffing the pavement, kicking pebbles just because it felt right. He still forgot his homework from time to time, and he still imagined wild stories.

But the stories had changed; they were brave adventures, and he was now part of those stories. He carried the dragon-glass arrowhead around his neck. Sometimes, when he had a hard day or the world felt too big, he'd close his eyes and remember. He did not tell anyone about the dagger Morwyn had given him, or the Dragon who watched from places just beyond sight. He didn't need to. Leadership, he had learned, was not about being seen.

Even his teachers noticed his newfound confidence. His classmates noticed the spark in his smile, too. Aaron was still a child. But he was no longer small.

Ray

Ray still ran his morning trash route, big hands lifting bins with ease, boots crunching over pavement. But people looked at him differently now, children even greeted him or approached him with questions, so when a frightened child from down the block asked, "Mr. Ray, are monsters real?" Ray crouched, smiled gently, and said, "Sometimes. But so are good people who stop them."

He'd found a small group of friends now, Claire, Sage, Jonas, Aaron, and Morwyn, who met every month at the coffee shop. They laughed. They talked. And Ray's grief, once a heavy stone in his chest, slowly softened.

The shield of the Weave still lived with him, resting against the wall of his garage, polished and ready. Some things were meant to be held quietly; he still wore the leather wrap all the time as a reminder of the things he had seen and experienced

When danger or fear brushed close, his instinct sharpened. His courage steadied. Ray finally understood: He wasn't just a protector in the realm. He had always been one, here too, he still found things in the trash that made him pause, a coiled piece of metal, a scrap of parchment, a small carved stone. He never threw those things away, he is and always will remain a collector and protector.

Sage

Sage's studio changed. The walls are filled with art, all complete and perfect in their own way. They stopped erasing so much. Stopped waiting for the line to explain itself. They trusted their hand; they let the work become what it wanted to be, and creativity flowed.

People who purchased their art did so because it felt alive. And they were right. Galleries began asking to show their work: pieces depicting impossible places, strange forests, spiraling towers, and one mysterious arch carved with five symbols. The graphite shard they were given sat neatly in its pouch, not often used now but ready and waiting when direction or answers were needed.

They painted with the knowledge that creation mattered, even if only to a handful of souls. One evening, Sage looked up from a charcoal sketch of a dragon sitting by a boy's side. And, for just a moment… they could have sworn a warm gust of gold brushed past their cheek.

Jonas

Jonas returned to the corner where he played violin each morning. The old guitar case, sarcastic and temperamental as ever, sat open at his feet. He played often. Sometimes for passersby. Sometimes for the spaces between things

But something had changed. A young woman approached him one morning and said, your music makes me feel like I'm not alone." Jonas nodded, a gentle smile lifting at the corners. "Then it's doing its job."

And every so often, Jonas paused mid-tune, head tilting as if listening for something distant. A whisper. When that happened, he smiled and played a little louder.

Morwyn

Morwyn's coffee shop remained exactly the same: warm, fragrant, and always glowing as though lit from the inside. She poured tea, honey cakes, and continued to listen.

But now she watched her five visitors with quiet pride whenever they arrived, five threads she had long known would someday awaken. And each time, she whispered blessings under her breath, ancient, gentle, effective because she knew the shift would come again, as long as there were greedy people on this earth, and creatures who wanted to rule it all in the unseen realms, things would change and become unstable once again, and when those worlds shifted, she would be ready.

When Aaron once asked her if she ever missed "the other realm," Morwyn smiled, eyes shimmering with centuries of knowledge.

"My boy," she said kindly, "I don't miss it. I walk with it always."

The Red Door

By late spring, vines had begun to grow up the ancient frame of the Red Door, weaving themselves in patterns that almost resembled the five symbols.

Passersby still saw it as odd, old, or quaint. But to those who had entered it, it vibrated with quiet knowing.

Every night, when the street grew still, the Red Door glowed faintly with the silver sheen of the restored Weave. It was patient, just watching.

One evening, as the sun dipped low, the door creaked open just an inch as if stretching after a long sleep. The wind rustled, the threads shimmered, and something whispered across the air: "Until I am needed again." Then the Red Door closed tightly once again.

THE END

Or, perhaps… The beginning of another thread.